Indy caught her breath.

It was him. *The Beast.*

"Hello, Mr. Gilbert. It's nice to meet you."

"Hello, Rosalinda."

She furrowed her brow at hearing her given name but smiled at him.

"Why did you challenge me?" he asked.

He was even better looking in person. The scar on the side of his face just added to his appeal, making him look dangerous in a safe-but-sexy way. He was taller than she'd expected as well, and compared to her five foot five inches, he was about a foot taller than her.

There was a leashed power in him that made the air around him almost crackle and she felt a shiver down her spine.

He looked like a man who took what he wanted.

* * *

One Night Wager by Katherine Garbera is part of The Gilbert Curse series.

Dear Reader,

I'm so excited to bring you the first book in The Gilbert Curse series! I have always loved fairy tales and remember the first time I saw Disney's *Beauty and the Beast*. A heroine who reads and has brown hair and brown eyes—finally one who I could really identify with—and of course, a beastly hero has always been a favorite of mine.

Conrad Gilbert was so much fun to write. I think that the high-pressure world of the celebrity chef sort of lends itself easily to a man who comes across as a beast. It's one of the few areas where everything has to be finished at an exact time and Conrad is used to everyone listening to him.

Indy isn't one for taking orders, but she is determined to do whatever it takes to break the "curse" that the town council is sure the town has. If that means facing the beast in the kitchen and then making a risky wager, so be it.

I hope you enjoy the results of their *One Night Wager*!

Happy reading!

Katherine

KATHERINE GARBERA

ONE NIGHT WAGER

Recycling programs for this product may not exist in your area.

ISBN-13: 978-1-335-58172-3

One Night Wager

This is a work of fiction. Names, characters, places and incidents are either the product of the author's imagination or are used fictitiously. Any resemblance to actual persons, living or dead, businesses, companies, events or locales is entirely coincidental.

For questions and comments about the quality of this book, please contact us at CustomerService@Harlequin.com.

Harlequin Enterprises ULC
22 Adelaide St. West, 41st Floor
Toronto, Ontario M5H 4E3, Canada
www.Harlequin.com

Printed in U.S.A.

Katherine Garbera is the *USA TODAY* bestselling author of more than a hundred and twenty-five books. Her award-winning books are known for their emotional intensity and sizzling sensuality. She lives in the midlands of the UK with her husband. She loves to connect with readers online at www.katherinegarbera.com and on Facebook, Instagram and Twitter.

Books by Katherine Garbera

Harlequin Desire

The Image Project

Billionaire Makeover
The Billionaire Plan
Billionaire Fake Out

The Gilbert Curse

One Night Wager

Visit the Author Profile page
at Harlequin.com for more titles.

You can also find Katherine Garbera on Facebook,
along with other Harlequin Desire authors,
at Facebook.com/HarlequinDesireAuthors!

This book is dedicated to my good friend
Joss Wood, a wonderful writer and also a good
person, who's always there when I need her.

Acknowledgment:

Thank you to John Jacobson for their
keen insight and deft editing of this book.
I am looking forward to working
on a lot of books together.

One

Conrad Gilbert didn't look like any beast she'd seen or envisioned. He had the sleeves of his chef's white jacket rolled up to reveal muscly forearms covered in a tattoo that, when the camera zoomed in, seemed to be thorny vines. His hands moved with speed and precision. When he looked up to speak to the viewer, Indy Belmont shivered with sensual awareness which warned her it had been too long since she'd gone out on a date or had a hookup. She wasn't listening to a single word that came out of that perfectly formed masculine mouth.

She wanted to kiss him. She wanted to feel those big arms wrapped around her, with him saying her name in that deep timbre of his that reminded her of long, hot summer nights.

"So what do you think?" Lilith Montgomery, the head of the Main Street Business Alliance and the woman in charge of this endeavor, asked as she hit Pause on the video screen. Leaving Conrad's face zoomed in, looking intently out at Indy.

"Huh?" Indy asked, realizing her father would roll his eyes at the comment. She'd come to Gilbert Corners at the town council's invitation. Her show *Hometown, Home Again* had taken off over the last season and now that Lansdowne was revitalized, her producers had been looking for another town in need of her skills. "Sorry. He's very intense."

"He is. Even as a youth he was. So can you get him to come to town and break the curse?" Jeff Hamilton asked.

Indy smiled and nodded with confidence. They were on the same network, so getting Conrad to come to Gilbert Corners should be easy. Her best friend was from Gilbert Corners and had bought and opened a coffee shop here, and Indy herself wasn't too bad in the kitchen.

"I can get him here. What's this about a curse?"

Lilith shook her head. "It's just sad. Gilbert International closed their main factory, and the very next weekend the three Gilbert heirs were in a horrific car crash."

"One boy-Declan Owen-was left dead and two of the heirs near death. After that the town started drying up."

"When was this?" Indy asked not sure she believed in the curse.

"Ten years ago."

About the time that inflation, combined with the economic downturn, made it hard for small businesses to stay afloat in small towns like this—where college kids went away and didn't come back. She suspected that had more to do with vacant shops on Main Street than a curse. But a curse would make good TV.

"I'd say that curse has run long enough. I can do it," she said. Though she had no specific plan. She'd learned that the only way to make things happen was to believe she could do them. "Are we sure getting him to come and do a cook-off in the town is what we need?"

She'd moved to the town of Gilbert Corners eighteen months ago when she'd purchased a failing bookshop and a fixer-upper Victorian house off the main town square. She had done something similar in her hometown after college. She'd started as a YouTuber with a small following, trying desperately to fix up the house she'd inherited as a way to find some peace with the woman she had become. Viewers had responded and she'd ended up with a massive following when the offer to do her own television show on the Home Living channel had come in. That was two years ago, and once she'd gotten the business thriving and the town back on the path to its former glory, she'd needed a new project. Especially since her partner—and the man she'd been crushing on forever—had fallen in love with someone else and married her.

Renovating the Main Street, breaking a curse and getting over her past seemed like a big ask and she knew she had her work cut out for her.

Gilbert Corners was close enough to Boston that it should be a booming commuting suburb but instead it had definitely seen better days.

"It's a start," Lilith said. "Do you think you can do it?"

Indy, who had been called obstinate and been told that she never gave up, wasn't worried about that. "No problem."

She left town hall and walked back across the park where weeds had choked out the once beautiful flower beds. Graffiti covered the base of the statue that honored the four founding fathers of Gilbert Corners who'd helped during the American Revolution. She entered her bookshop, Indy's Treasures, and waved at Kym, the high school student who helped out in the afternoons, as she entered her office at the back.

Conrad Gilbert, celebrity chef known as the Beast. She pulled up his online profile.

He had thick dark curly hair that framed his face. His brows were thick and his eyes were an icy blue. He had a long jagged scar down his left cheek ending at the top of his lip. He wore a chef's jacket but above the collar she saw ink from a tattoo that went around his neck. His arms were crossed over his chest.

Who dares challenge the Beast in his lair?

The words were emblazoned under his crossed arms. She read further and saw that he accepted cooking challenges from across North America to be televised on his show. There was a place to enter information to challenge him. He'd come to the town of the challenger and they would go head-to-head making a famous local or regional dish.

"Yes!"

"Yes, what? I heard you agreed to get the Beast to come to town."

She glanced up as Nola Weston, her best friend and the reason she had come to Gilbert Corners, walked into her office. When Indy had been starting out on YouTube, Nola, her former college roommate and self-taught woodworker, had joined her team. Nola set her mug of coffee on the desk, leaning against it.

"I did. I mean, he's not *really* a beast, and I think it would be good to have a Gilbert to return to town."

"Why didn't you go for Dash? He visits all the time to see his sister at the sanatorium."

"Conrad has a TV show which will get us some national exposure, plus Lilith thought he'd be the easier of the two."

"The Beast, easier? They play it up on TV, but he's a very arrogant and kind of just does what he wants. I'm not sure he'll help you."

"Oh, he'll say yes," Indy said. Nola was skeptical, but Indy was confident. *The Beast's Lair* was a competition show where he accepted the challenges of amateur chefs and if they beat him they were awarded a $350,000 prize. That money would go a long way toward fixing up Gilbert Corners.

She filled in the application and used her grandmother's Low Country Boil recipe, something which she had made a few times on her show for the crew and had gotten rave reviews.

Two days later she heard back from her contact at the network that her application for Gilbert Corners to be featured on *The Beast's Lair* had been accepted.

After closing her email, Indy sat back in the leather chair that had been her grandfather's and started making plans. *Real plans.* They'd need to clean up the park and get the graffiti off the statue, but she was excited...which she told herself had nothing to do with meeting the Beast in person.

"No."

Conrad Gilbert didn't suffer fools or repeat himself. He put down the bottle of garlic-infused olive oil he'd been holding and turned to look at Ophelia Burnetti who was the executive producer on his food television show.

"You can't say no. I've already told them you're coming."

"Well you can tell them I'm not." Conard Gilbert didn't even bother looking up from his bench as he worked on the delicate design for the plating of his latest dish. His new assistant was going to be fired. He hated being disturbed when he was in his test kitchen, and everyone knew it.

"Con, this is happening. Gilbert Corners is close by and we need to fill the vacancy left by the unusable video we shot at the Kentucky Derby."

"It's not unusable."

"The other chef had a meltdown and threw a bottle of bourbon at you. It would ruin him. This place is close, and they want you to film in less than three weeks. It's ideal."

He straightened to his full six foot five inches, giving her a withering stare. She looked back at him nonplussed.

Fuck.

He'd vowed to never return to Gilbert Corners except to visit his cousin Rory. And he didn't want to break that vow now. He hated that place.

"If I go, I'll arrive as the cooking starts and then leave as soon as we are done filming."

"Fine. I only need forty minutes of airable footage. So do that and you're out."

Ophelia left a few minutes later after telling him she'd send the details to his assistant. Conrad followed her out into the main office area where his assistant sat doing something on her cell phone.

"Send it to me," Conrad said to Ophelia, turning to his assistant. "You're fired."

He walked back into the test kitchen, but his mind was no longer on the dish he'd been creating. It was on fucking Gilbert Corners. He had no happy memories of the town that bore his family's name. His grandfather had been a cold, demanding guardian who'd raised Conrad and his cousins after their parents were killed in an airplane crash as they'd been returning from a ski trip. Conrad had been ten.

He'd never felt like Gilbert Manor was home. He had missed his actual home—the brownstone that had been in his mother's family, where he'd lived with his parents. He'd been loved and treated like their little prince and their deaths had left him empty. His grandfather had taken one look at Conrad and his two cousins when they'd shown up on his doorstep and immediately arranged for them to be sent off to boarding schools. He and Dash, who was like a brother to him, had been sent to the same one.

He reached for his phone and called Dash.

"Gilbert here."

"Gilbert here," he responded.

"Con, how's it going?" Dash asked.

"I have to go to GC."

"You have to? I thought no one dared tell you what to do."

"Me too. But Ophelia isn't scared of me, and we need an episode to fill a programming gap. Why would anyone invite me to town?" Conrad asked.

"You got me. They all think we're bad luck."

"Exactly. Well, I'm going to crush the challenger and then get out of GC. Want to join me?"

"Hell no. I visit Gilbert Corners' care home once a week and that's enough for me."

"How's Rory?" he asked.

Conrad rubbed his face. His scar was a constant reminder of the past but he'd learned to live with it. So much of who he'd been had been lost on that night. But the truth was, he was luckier than Dash and Rory, and he knew it.

He'd often thought that the crash had just brought his true self to the surface. His grandfather had wanted to have a plastic surgeon fix the scar but Conrad had refused. He was tired of playing the old man's game. The scar had reshaped him. And he had no regrets.

"She's the same. Her doctor is retiring. I need to be in GC to talk to the new doctor taking over. When are you going?"

"I'll send the date when I have it," he said. They hung up and he turned back to the bench where he'd been working earlier.

He wanted to smash something at the thought of having to return to Gilbert Corners. It didn't matter that his grandfather had died almost eight years ago; he would always associate that town with the old man.

Ophelia forwarded him the information on his challenger, Rosalinda Belmont. He looked her up and saw that she had recently moved to town and had her own television show *Hometown, Home Again* on the same network his show was on.

He clicked on the promo video of her new program in Gilbert Corners. She had dark hair and a heart-shaped face. She wore glasses in her photo and had a book in her hands. She walked through the bookshop on Main Street in front of a sign that read Indy's Treasures; underneath it was the slogan "Adventure is just one book away."

Conrad never went into a challenge uninformed so he forwarded her information to a private investigator.

He looked down at her big brown eyes, felt something stir inside of him. Part sexual, part curiosity, part something he couldn't define. He just wished he knew what she was up to.

"So...someone was in town asking about you yesterday," Nola said as Indy stopped by Java Juice the next morning. "I don't like it."

"Ha. I'm sure it was nothing. Maybe that wealthy king and queen finally realized where they left me," Indy said as she handed Nola her thermal to-go coffee mug.

"Your sweet parents would be devastated to hear you say that."

"Naw, I promised to cut them in on my fortune once I'm found," she said with a wink. She wasn't too concerned about anyone asking after her. She had nothing to hide.

The morning rush was over and the tables of the coffee shop were filled with the usual suspects. Simone, who was working on her doctoral thesis, Pete, who was planning the next quest for his Dungeons & Dragons group, and then the young moms in the back enjoying some adult conversation while their toddlers played next to them.

Nola prepared Indy's normal order of a large Americano with skim milk. "Would you mind if I put a flyer on your bulletin board asking for some help weeding in the park on Saturday? I want to try to get the park in better shape before the cooking competition. I mean, the town council should do it but..."

"They're busy paying for things like road repair and other community needs."

Indy turned to see Jeff Hamilton behind her. He smiled at her. "I know, but we need to make this place look nice."

"The park is on the list, but there are so many things that need to be done," Jeff said. "My wife, June, owns the nursery on the outskirts of town. I can talk to her about bringing plants for the bedding. Did you find a sponsor yet?"

"Not yet, I'm still in talks with one of the sponsors I use on my show. But Conrad Gilbert is coming to town on May 1 to film his show. Once I win, we'll have a nice amount of money to put toward it. I'm going to use that to get more people involved. It is a long road but we will get there."

"I'm impressed. How did you convince him to do that?" Jeff asked.

"I contacted his show and challenged him to a cook-off here."

"You did?"

"Yes. I think this challenge will be good," she said.

She wanted everyone to see the beauty she did in Gilbert Corners. She loved the old Victorian architecture that dominated the vacant buildings on Main Street. When she walked down Main Street, she saw so much potential in the town and wanted them to realize it.

She talked to Nola and Jeff about which shop they should renovate next and made some notes before she took her coffee from Nola and left. She opened the bookshop and enjoyed the light foot traffic that came in. She loved the smell of the books and discussing her favorite titles with clients.

She casually brought up Conrad Gilbert with her customers and found out that he'd been considered devastatingly handsome before the accident, spoiled and arrogant. One of her customers said that he'd acted like the town of Gilbert Corners was below his social standing. Interesting.

She hadn't thought it would come so quickly, but on the first of May, she packed up her ingredients and her courage and headed to Gilbert Manor, following the cobblestone road that went over a quaint stone bridge that spanned the brackish-water river that flowed through Gilbert Corners.

She was nervous as she hauled her ingredients to the tent she was directed to. She felt someone watching her. The figure inside the tent was backlit by the sun. He had broad shoulders that practically filled the tent frame and wore a leather jacket. As he moved more across the yard, she caught her breath as she recognized him. The Beast.

She patted her hair and smoothed her hands down the sides of the fitted Bardot top she wore before she realized that made her look nervous and stopped.

"Hello there, Mr. Gilbert. It's nice to meet you," she said.

"Hello, Rosalinda."

She furrowed her brow at hearing her given name but smiled at him. "No one calls me Rosalind. I'm

Indy. Indy Belmont." She kept talking because he stood there, sort of glaring at her but not full-on glaring. It made her nervous.

"What's up?" she asked.

"Why did you challenge me?" he responded.

"Oh, well, I'm not sure if you know it or not, but people in this town believe there is a curse that involves your family. It's keeping business away and slowly killing the town," she said. "I have a show where—"

"I know about your show," he said.

"Oh, do you watch it?"

She wasn't nervous now. He was even better looking in person. The scar on the side of his face just added to his appeal, making him look dangerous in a safe-but-sexy way. He was taller than she'd expected as well, and compared to her five foot five inches he was about a foot taller than her.

There was a leashed power in him that made the air around him almost crackle and she felt a shiver down her spine. He looked like a man who took what he wanted. Not that anyone would say no to him. He was watching her so keenly that she was hyperaware of her body and her femininity. She didn't feel threatened or unsafe—just seen. Seen in a way that she hadn't been in a long time.

She pushed her glasses up on her nose and gave him another smile as he stood there, still watching her.

"Want to grab some coffee before we start filming and I'll give you the details?"

"No. Tell me what you know about the curse," he said in a grumbly voice.

"Does this brooding asshole thing work for you?" she asked. Realizing he was just going to keep pushing unless she put a stop to it.

"I prefer to think of myself as laser focused rather than asshole."

"I guess that's in the eyes of the beholder," she said, turning and walking away.

Two

In person, Rosalinda Belmont was more vibrant than he'd expected. That video hadn't captured her vitality at all. She'd looked slightly rough-around-the-edges. In person she glowed. She had long curly hair which she wore at the top of her head in a high ponytail. She had a curvy figure revealed by high-waisted sailor-style jeans and a plain three-quarter-length-sleeve ballet top.

He was still annoyed with the way she dismissed him.

"She's cute. Actually, this whole town is. Remind me again why you hate it," his sous chef, Rita, said, interrupting his thoughts as she joined him at his bench.

He ignored the comment because it wasn't any of her business and directed her to get the prep done before he moved off to check on the rest of the mise en place for cooking.

He hated this town because it reminded him of who he had been. How he'd looked down on the townspeople as not being as good as he was. He had hated mingling with them, something his grandfather had reinforced.

The accident had changed all of that, and being back here stirred too much of the man he'd been. He didn't like it.

Conrad was familiar with the setup of the tent as it was always the same and set to his preferences. Ophelia made sure he had a bench where he could work by himself, and that Rita was set to the left side where she could hand him things and be filmed doing her part.

He noticed that Ms. Belmont was chatting with another woman with short red hair and a rounded face. She looked sort of familiar like maybe he'd known her when he'd grown up in Gilbert Corners. But he wasn't interested in renewing any acquaintances; he wanted to do this cook and get out of here.

She glanced over and waved at him before walking toward him. He stood where he was, sharpening the knives he planned to use during the show because he knew a lot of home chefs found that intimidating.

"Sorry for losing my temper with you earlier. I just really don't deal well with…beasts," she said with a flash of a gamine grin that sent a bolt of heat through him.

"No problem. You were right—I was being an ass.

Normally my challengers refer to me as Chef Gilbert, not The Beast."

She laughed. A light, tinkling sound that he noticed drew the attention of several of the production crew, which annoyed him.

"Did you need anything else?" he asked, hating that she was a distraction.

"Are you always this brusque?"

He arched one eyebrow. There was something unsettling about her, and he wished it made it easier for him to ignore the attraction between them. But it didn't. He was half aroused from this exchange.

"So that's a yes," she said with a sigh.

"GC brings out the worst in me. I was actually surprised that you wanted to do the challenge here. Why did you?"

"The curse."

He groaned. "Of course. You don't really believe the local legend that if a Gilbert returns then the town will flourish again?" he asked drily.

"Oh, well…yeah. I mean, the publicity from being on your show won't hurt either. I wasn't sure you knew about the curse," she said. "I was hoping we could have lunch after and discuss—"

"Let me stop you there. I'm here for the few hours it's going to take to film this and them I'm gone. There is nothing that interests me in Gilbert Corners."

She tipped her head to the side and narrowed her eyes. "Not even your cousin at the GC Care Facility?"

He shook his head and put down the large knife he'd been sharpening as he leaned toward her, using all of his height and the menace of his scarred face and body to intimidate her. "Is that all?"

She swallowed; he saw her throat work, and she frowned for a minute before putting her hands on her hips. "You're not a very nice man, are you?"

"I don't have to be, I'm the Beast."

"Tell you what, Beast, I'll wager a weekend of having you help out around town that I can beat you at this competition."

"What's in it for me?"

"The gratitude of the people of Gilbert Corners."

He rolled his eyes. "I meant what do I get if I win?"

Her hands dropped and she chewed her lower lip for a moment. "What do you want?"

As soon as she said that, an image of her naked on his bed flashed into his head, but he knew that wasn't something he could say out loud. "You, for one romantic weekend."

He saw a flush move up her neck to her cheeks.

"Me?" she squeaked.

"Yup. Take it or leave it."

He had no doubt that she was going to be dropping her wager faster than a hot dish. She'd made a bold move and he'd countered. He turned back to check the other tools in his chef's kit figuring that was the end of the conversation, but he felt the light touch of her hand on his forearm.

Another jolt of fire went straight through his body making his blood feel like it was flowing heavier in his veins.

"Okay."

"Okay?"

"I accept your wager. Winner gets a weekend. You get romance, I get you volunteering and working around town," she said. "Deal?"

He looked into those large brown eyes of hers and wondered what was so special about this town that she was willing to go through so much to try to get him to come back here. She held her hand out to him. Was it just her show? This felt more important, more personal to her than just a television show.

"Why is Gilbert Corners so important to you?" he asked.

"I hate to see a beautiful town like this abandoned and forgotten. We should be taking care of our past and our history," she said.

That didn't really answer his question. He felt the same way about older city centers and buildings. He hated to see them torn down for new construction and had opened his Michelin-starred restaurant in an old sewing factory in Brooklyn.

"Nice sentiment, but what's in it for you?"

"You're persistent. I like that. I guess you'll have to win the wager if you want to find out," she said.

"You know I've earned three Michelin stars over the course of my career, right?"

She nodded, crossing her arms under her breasts as if to say "so what."

"Just wanted to give you a heads-up that you're probably not winning," he said.

"Or maybe I have a dish that will tame the Beast," she countered.

Interesting. He was going to win the wager and have Indy in his bed for one long weekend.

Indy hadn't expected him to be so overwhelming in person.

His for 48 hours. That sounded…like too much to unpack before she was meant to cook in the Beast's Lair and win.

The way he'd issued what he'd claim had a sent a shiver down her spine. It didn't help matters that her hand still tingled from where she'd touched him. He was solid.

If his eyes had been bright blue in the photos online, in person, they were even more brilliant. She couldn't stop looking at him. He rattled her.

But. She had a plan. She just had to stick to it. She'd been making *Hometown, Home Again* for three years. After the incident at college, she'd come home and become a sort of shut-in, remote learning and avoiding everyone until her parents had bought a small bookshop and asked her to refurbish the dilapidated building. She'd made YouTube videos as a way of documenting the project at first, but also, she knew, to find her voice again.

At first her audience was small and that was fine. She'd made the videos for herself. But then it had started to grow and the TV offer had come in. For the last few years she'd been fixing up every building in her own hometown. Fixing something so she didn't have to focus on the parts of her that probably could use some work.

If she could revitalize Gilbert Corners and draw in some big developers, it would be another feather in her cap. It was her dream. She liked the bookshop she ran and she got a lot of her ideas for the town from stories she'd read. She saw the potential in Gilbert Corners, and if she had to spend a weekend with Chef Gilbert to get it, she'd do it.

He faced her, raising both eyebrows at her. "Are you sure? I'm willing to let you back out if you want to. Once we start cooking, I won't."

"I'm sure," she said. "I'd never renege. That's not the kind of person I am."

He tipped his head to one side, his gaze moving down her body, awakening things she was just going to ignore. "I can see that."

"Good. So a handshake will seal the deal?"

He hesitated and then reluctantly held his hand out to her. She reached out, steeling herself to touch him again. The warmth of him enfolded her before his grip did. His hand was bigger than hers and there were calluses on his fingers as they slid along the back of her hand. He held it firmly, professionally, but she still felt that traitorous feminine awareness shiver up her arm.

She pumped their hands up and down and then pulled hers back as if she'd touched a hot poker.

He didn't say anything, just raised his eyebrows again. She licked her lips and then turned to walk back to her cooking station.

"Anything else?" she asked, trying for a calmness that she'd honestly never had. But the chance to get him to stay in town longer than the few hours it would take to cook was perfect. She tried to distract herself from him by thinking of the three things she'd ask him to do.

"Nope. Good luck."

"I have skill. I don't need luck."

"Your ego… I can't wait for this competition to start," she said.

"That eager to be mine?" he asked.

She flushed again and ignored it. "I'm eager to show you off around town. I can't wait to see the excitement of everyone here when you host a spring gala at Gilbert Manor."

"Dream on," he said.

She tried to be cool as she looked at the back bench where she needed to start chopping vegetables to get prepped for the cook-off. Nola raised both eyebrows at her.

"What was that about?"

"I…"

Oh God. Now that she was looking at the ingredients she'd prepared for her version of a New England clam chowder, she wasn't sure she could win, but she was damned determined to try. She had tested out the dish a few times on her production crew. But they weren't Michelin-star judges. Maybe she shouldn't have made the wager, but she'd always had a problem with impulse control.

Why hadn't see just reasoned with him?

"You?" Nola asked again.

She took a deep breath and then decided to sound

confident. The judges of the cook-off were made up of a professional chef from a neighboring town—Tony Elton, town council member Jeff Hamilton, and three randomly selected people from the audience. There was a chance she could win, she told herself. They had mics on, but the production assistant had shown them how to turn them off and on. She double-checked—hers was off.

"Is your mic off?"

Nola looked at hers and flicked it to off. "Yes… but girl, you are worrying me."

"I made a side wager on the outcome of the cooking challenge. And if I win, he has to stay in town for an entire weekend."

"And if he wins?"

She waved her hand toward her friend. "Doesn't matter. I'm not going to lose."

Nola nodded. "Glad to hear it. Either way, you might be in trouble. You don't want to spend a weekend with the Beast."

"Why not?"

Nola looked around to make sure no one was near them, but then still leaned in close, making Indy very worried.

"Rumor has it he's very hard to resist one-on-one. I heard that he goes through a woman a weekend, and they aren't complaining when they leave."

"Nola. He's not interested in me that way," she said, lying to her friend since he'd specifically mentioned a romantic weekend. "He just said that to make me back down."

"Which you didn't. So let's face it, Indy, you're the next delicious morsel on his plate."

She blushed and shook her head again. "Stop it. That's not going to happen."

"We will see," Nola said. "I guess we need to start getting ready to cook, right?"

"Yes."

Nola moved away and Indy looked down at the cooler with her ingredients in it. She hadn't allowed herself to dwell on what would happen if he won. But surely, he knew he couldn't just demand things from her?

Who said he'd have to?

She ignored her inner voice as her eyes strayed over to his cooking station and she saw him with his head down, chopping. He wasn't interested in her. Men seemed to take one look at her and relegate her to the sweet girl next-door. That wasn't the kind of woman a man asked to spend the weekend in his bed. But there was a part of her that wished that was what he'd meant. It would be nice to be the sexy one instead of the smart, reliable one. Just once.

Ophelia waved Conrad and Indy over about forty-five minutes later. The townspeople of Gilbert Corners had come out for the competition which Dash had agreed they could hold on the grounds of Gilbert Manor. The large mansion loomed in the background.

The octagonal tower element at the front elevation made the mansion look welcoming but still grand.

The columns and traditional architectural elements on either side of the steps leading to the main entrance added formality to the more laid-back authentic cedar-shingle roof that lent a natural aspect to the mansion and complemented it with an aged soft silver-gray color. There was a porte cochere that the production vans were parked underneath. Locals in attendance had left their cars in the large paved side lot that had always been used for these types of events.

But Conrad knew that no local, save those employed by the Gilbert Manor foundation, had been here since the night of the winter ball that had changed his life and led the town to believe they were cursed.

The classic red brick and Tennessee fieldstone chimney was visible from the backyard where the competition was being held. The audience had entered through a lovely garden gate to the covered rear terrace where Ophelia's team had set up seating for them. There were lattice walls on one side that served as a wind block but let in sunlight.

Conrad had offered to allow Indy to use the outdoor dining area adjacent to the covered lounge, but Ophelia had insisted they use the exact same setup. Stated that the judging would only be fair if they both were using the studio-provided kitchen areas.

"Before we get started, Ms. Belmont, I wanted to make sure you had everything you needed?"

Indy smiled at Ophelia, and he couldn't help noticing the difference between the two women. Ophelia was tall and sleek, carrying herself with a cool sophistication that made Indy seem sort of small-town and…charming. Which just reinforced that his mind was on the wager. He seldom lost a cook-off—in fact, the last time he had, it had been to a master chef who earned his first Michelin star when he was eighteen.

"I think I have everything. One of your assistants showed me how to use the pressure cooker you provided, so I should be good," she said.

He wondered what she was using the pressure cooker for. The cook-off was traditional coastal recipes. He knew that Indy had wanted to do a low country boil, but they had to cook the same dish, so the producers had decided on a traditional New England clam chowder instead. The littleneck clams had been locally sourced from the neighboring town of Calm Bay. There was no time limit on the cook, so she wouldn't be under pressure to get her dish up fast.

He looked over at her and wondered if he should go and give her some advice. He glanced at her bench and made a few notes before realizing what he was doing. He didn't want to spend more time in GC and if he helped her…

"Chef Gilbert?" Ophelia asked.

"I'm good," Conrad said, turning his attention to his friend and away from the tempting Indy. He reminded himself he didn't like anyone associated with Gilbert Corners.

It was just a bit hard since she stood to his right smelling like summer and making him think about what she would look like after he kissed her.

"Great. So, just to run through this. I'll do an intro with both of you and then you will go to your stations. Don't do anything until the cameraman assigned to you is in position and our director, CJ, will tell you to start. I will bring the judges by and let them ask you questions about your cook as it's going on. Don't worry about anything you say—we will edit the footage later so if you don't want to talk or can't talk, that's fine," Ophelia said.

"What will they be asking?" Indy wanted to know.

Indy was starting to look a little nervous. Conrad almost smiled to himself. He had almost forgotten he was back in Gilbert Corners now.

"Just things like 'what are you doing' and 'how did you come up with the recipe,'" Ophelia said. "Are you ready?"

"Yes."

"As I'll ever be," Indy said, which made Ophelia smile.

"Don't worry, Ms. Belmont, once you start cooking, you'll forget the cameras are there just like on your own show. Let me introduce you both to today's judges and then we'll get the filming going."

Ophelia waved over the local chef, who was one that Conrad hadn't met before, but he'd looked him up and thought he sounded interesting. Jeff Hamilton was his age and they'd met a few times when Conrad had been home on summer break. The locals consisted of three people, with only one person that Conrad had never met before.

After they were introduced, Ophelia checked everyone's mics and then moved to a platform that had been set up. The audience coordinator had already warmed up the crowd and had given them instructions on what to do when Ophelia greeted them. Still, Conrad was surprised by the loud cheers from the locals.

"A love of the traditional and a fierce spirit of competition have brought The Beast back to his hometown and Gilbert Manor. The stakes are high for The Beast. He hasn't lost a cook-off in the last twelve challenges. Will this be his lucky thirteenth win?

"Or will newcomer and local resident Rosalinda 'Indy' Belmont defeat The Beast and send him back to his lair? Let's find out in this traditional *New England Clam Chowder Cook-off*."

The crowd cheered again and the director called cut. Stepped down and motioned them over to her. "Conrad, go and do your thing."

He stepped onto the platform, crossed his arms and waited for the cameraman to get in place before he glared menacingly into the lens. They did a few different takes and then it was Indy's turn.

"What should I do?" she asked him. "I'm a home cook not a tv chef. I know I have my show and I should be a natural in front of the camera but this is...different."

"I'd say your strength is that charming smile of yours, and your quirkiness. Just smile and feel authentic. Actually...where's Nola?"

"Why?"

"Because you will feel awkward just smiling at

the camera—believe me, it takes a bit to get used to it. If she stands behind the cameraman, you can smile at her."

"Thanks," she said.

"No problem. TV is an odd beast."

"Just like you," she quipped.

"Indeed."

He stepped back as she filmed her part. She intrigued him—part of it was that he hated being back on the grounds of the old man's home and seeing so many of the townspeople who were looking at him. Did they resent him for not coming back? They called it a curse, but he couldn't help feeling they blamed all of the Gilberts for the town losing residents and business.

Rubbing the back of his neck, he couldn't help thinking about Indy. Challenging him to break a curse supposedly but he knew there had to be more. And he couldn't wait to find out what it was.

Three

Indy had practiced making clam chowder, but this was different. This wasn't a frame she'd rescued from an estate sale that had languished in an attic for decades that was worn, maybe broken, and needed her care to restore it. This was a bunch of fresh ingredients, and for a moment she felt the beginning of a panic attack.

On her show she was always able to focus on what she was fixing because it was usually just her and a small crew, but here she felt the pressure of the townspeople watching her in real time.

Nola looked at her and took a deep breath, then nodded at her. Indy smiled at her friend and took a deep breath too. She could smell the garlic that she'd chopped a few minutes ago and the smokiness of the grills on the fire that she'd started.

These scents soothed her. She nodded to herself, blocking out everything but the ingredients on her bench. She was able to start cooking the chowder while the cameramen walked around her station and took different shots. Though Conrad had said that she'd forget the cameras were there, she didn't. But she'd figured out how to make it manageable.

Nola was her cooking assistant and was busily peeling and dicing the russet potatoes she was using in the recipe. Meanwhile Indy was on the clams. Because of the nature of this cook-off and the high stakes, she believed she had the best chance of winning by bringing out the freshness of the clams so she was steaming them in a wine-and-garlic sauce that she would later use to cook the bacon in.

Once the clams were steamed, she pulled them out. She sieved the remaining juice to get rid of any dirt that might have come from the clams. Then she had to shell them, which wasn't that hard since they had mostly all opened during the steaming.

Just as she felt like she was getting into a rhythm, Ophelia came over with a camera. "Ready for me?"

"Sure," she said with a confidence she was starting to feel. This curse-breaking business was more complicated than she'd anticipated. But her cook was going well.

"Is this recipe one of your own?" Ophelia asked.

"No, it's not. But I am bringing some techniques

and tastes from my grandmother's lessons. I thought this would be the perfect edge for me to use today."

"Interesting. That accent doesn't sound very New England," Ophelia said.

"No, ma'am, it's not, I'm from Georgia," Indy said.

"So are you bringing any Southern twists to your clam chowder today?"

Indy was. She'd texted her mom that morning and had decided to make some homemade cheddar biscuits that her mom was famous for to go with the clam chowder. "I am. I'm making my mama's biscuits. But also the using the basics I learned cooking low country boil growing up."

"Interesting. Why did you decide to do that?"

"Well the low country boil incorporates many of the same items as the clam chowder, so I thought the flavors might work together. If I'm going to beat the Beast, I needed to have something unique."

"Indeed. I'll leave you to your cooking," Ophelia said.

The director called cut. "That was great. You're a natural on camera."

"Thanks, this is so different from my show. I don't feel natural at all. Do I keep working?"

"Yes. Cut is just for interview part. We'll be bringing the judges through next. But keep cooking. There's a storm advisory and we're hoping to get these dishes finished before the rain arrives."

"How close is it?" Indy had gotten used to the storms that blew through this area off the Atlantic Ocean.

"We've got a couple of hours but not much more."

"Got it. I'll be done in time."

"Great," Ophelia said. "I'm the producer as well as host of this show, so I'm watching the budget. If we don't get this finished today, it'll be expensive to come back."

Ophelia smiled at her as she moved over to Conrad's station. Indy walked over to Nola who was still peeling the potatoes to give her the update.

"A storm's brewing. So chop faster I guess," Indy said.

"Of course there's a storm coming. The Beast is back in Gilbert Corners. It's just like that night ten years ago."

"Stop being overdramatic," Indy said.

"I wish I were. That night of the ball the day started perfect, like today, and then by midnight there was a blizzard. I'm just saying that *perhaps* something is trying to stop you from breaking the curse."

"I thought you didn't believe in it."

"I mean, of course I don't. But you have to admit, the weather's been pretty calm until he showed up."

"Maybe that means we *are* breaking the bad luck of this town. I mean, he's here," she said, moving back to her station to start cooking the bacon. She hadn't thought Nola was as invested in the curse as the others, but it seemed that not just the clam chowder was tradition.

The people of Gilbert Corners were going to read all kinds of bad omens into the storm. It made her realize why Conrad and his cousin Dashiell might not want to live here. But still, she thought, weather wasn't dictated by curses.

She felt someone watching her and glanced over at Conrad. Their stations were close enough for her to see his raised eyebrow and the frown that made the scar on the side of his face more pronounced. She caught her breath at how sexy he looked in his element. He might have been watching her, but his hands were still moving on the cutting board. There was a power in his movements and the way her watched her made her shiver with sensual awareness as he tossed something into his stockpot.

"Get busy," he said to her. "Unless you're that eager to be mine for a weekend that you're going to forfeit."

She realized she was just staring at him. "I'm right on track. Are you worried?"

"No."

She laughed at his comment.

"You should be. Indy is bringing some Southern heat to her dish," Ophelia said.

"Is she?"

"What, don't you think I can bring the heat?"

"Oh you're hot alright," he said.

She wasn't sure what he meant by that. She just went back to cooking, and the words continued drifting in and out of her mind as she tried to concentrate on her recipe. She'd felt a spark between them; she knew he had too. But she'd been trying to convince herself that when he'd asked for a weekend with her, it wasn't really going to be an intimate weekend. Now she wasn't so sure.

* * *

Conrad cooked on autopilot, which he knew wasn't a great idea when there were high stakes and a weekend with Indy was on the line, but he was distracted. He could blame it on being back in the one place he'd sworn to never return to, but he knew it was more than that.

Gilbert Manor was the problem.

No one had lived in the house for years, but the trust they'd dumped the inheritance they'd received from their grandfather into maintained the lawn and the house. He felt the stirring of anger, which he had always struggled to control when he was here. He might hate being back here but once he was cooking that all faded.

But he needed the distraction from Indy. She wasn't what he'd expected, and she had rattled him. He knew that he was coarse at times. He justified it by looking in the mirror, reminding himself of the jagged scar and the path he'd been on that had been taken from him in an instant.

But it wasn't the scar on his face that had changed him from the happy boy he'd been into this man. Gilbert Corners made him morose, and he hated that.

He dumped the ingredients into the stockpot and noticed that Rita was watching him.

"What?"

"You seem…"

He arched one eyebrow at her.

"Never mind."

Well, hell. He was distracted and he couldn't allow himself to be. Not today. He noticed some of the local judges were the Hammond sisters; Martha and Jean-Marie. They'd run the kitchens here at Gilbert Manor. Conrad knew he'd turned to cooking after the accident in part because of them.

"Ladies, it's nice to see you."

"You too, Con," Martha said. "It's been too long since a Gilbert was on these grounds."

"I'm not sure about that," he said drily.

"We've both missed you," Jean-Marie said.

"You two are part of the reason I'm a chef."

"We're flattered," Jean-Marie said with one of those sweet, sad smiles that he sometimes received from people who knew his past.

They asked him some questions about his dish, and he talked them through some of the changes he'd made to the basic recipe. He was using a fusion of Japanese cooking techniques that he'd been enjoying a lot lately and a classic French bisque, which was what the clam chowder was based on.

He couldn't help the soft spot he had for the sisters. The way they'd simply accepted him in their kitchens when he'd been hiding from his grandfather's rages. The way they'd directed him to the garden and told him about the edible plants and explained to him how flavor profiles worked.

Chasing away the last of the lust he'd felt for Indy, the somber feelings that being in this place stirred in him settled as the ladies moved on.

He continued putting in the ingredients and tasting the dish as it developed. Though he was ignoring her, he knew he wanted to win. He wanted her to be his for a weekend. And yeah, he could come back and ask her out, but that wasn't something he'd do. Once he won this wager, Gilbert Corners would see the last of him.

There was something more to Indy than met the eye. That spunky personality, those wide-leg pants and formfitting blouse. She moved around her kitchen tent in a flurry of movement that was precise, she was a very thorough woman, he realized, wondering if she was like that in every part of her life. The way she'd challenged him, then blushed, touched him and then pulled back.

He wanted her.

He shouldn't be turned on by a woman who lived in Gilbert Corners. But he was. And if his life had taught him one thing, it was that it was unpredictable and there was no guarantee for a long one.

He was going to have her.

"So this is what they pay you for?"

"Dash? What are you doing here?"

"He's a surprise judge," Ophelia said. "The locals were keen to have both of you here for the event."

"No wonder a storm's brewing," Conrad said.

Ophelia just shook her head. "I'm glad you were able to make it, Dash. I'll give you two a moment to catch up and then be back with the cameras."

Dash looked tired. The last ten years had been hardest on him. Though he'd been unscarred by the crash, he'd been the one to watch Conrad and Rory go through numerous operations and rehab. Rory was still in a coma.

"God, I still hate this place," Conrad said.

"Yeah, me too. I'm really surprised you agreed to do this," Dash said.

He told Dash about the alleged curse as he worked. Rita looked calmer now that he wasn't watching Indy, and their dish was starting to come together.

"So if you win the curse is broken? Or if she wins?" Dash asked.

"I don't think they even know. Folks around this part love a good legend. Apparently, the Main Street Business Alliance is going to use this cook-off to raise the town's profile, and Indy's got a TV show where she refurbishes run-down towns like GC."

"That sounds interesting. But still, I guess you better win."

"I always win."

"Of course you do—you're a Gilbert. I'll leave you to the cooking and go meet your competition."

Dash walked away but he couldn't help thinking about what his cousin had said. He was a Gilbert. The next forty minutes were intense as he finished his dish and the sourdough bread bowls to serve the chowder in. Ophelia told them when to end their cooking and then judges were moved into position at the table. The competition was judged blind, so both his and Indy's workstations had a partition set up as they plated the dishes, and then the servers would come and collect them.

The tables for plating were set back to back and he was very aware of the smell of summer peaches as she moved behind him. He finished and turned to see she was still working, but then she concluded and spun to face him.

"I think that's it," she said, wiping her hands on her curvy hips.

"It is. Now it's in the hands of fate," he said.

"Fate? You strike me as too cynical to believe in fate." She gave him that gamine smile of hers again as she tipped her head to the side to study him.

There was nothing sexual in the pose or the question, but he felt his cock stir. He wanted her. She wasn't his normal type. That dichotomy of confidence and nerves was usually too chaotic for him, but with Indy it seemed to be making him want her more. "I am, but it's right up your alley, isn't it?"

"Maybe," she said with a teasing grin.

"Maybe?"

"Yes. But I don't like the feeling I'm getting from you, that because I believe in fate I'm not grounded."

"I don't think that."

"What do you think?"

"That you believe in breaking curses and magical things. I don't," he said. "But that doesn't lessen you in my eyes."

Hell. This was why he shouldn't be here. Why had he said that?

It was the truth but still…he wished he'd kept it to himself. The sooner this competition was over and he was out of here, the better.

She knew he meant his words as a compliment and took them as one. She wiped her hands on her apron.

Nola and Conrad's assistant weren't in this staging area. It was just the two of them behind the partition as their dishes were taken out to be served.

"What happens now?"

"Nervous?"

"Since this entire thing started," she admitted. "You?"

"Not really."

"Of course not," she muttered. "Can I try yours?"

"Sure. I'm curious about yours as well. I'm not sure about your biscuits."

"Uh, that's my mama's recipe, Beast, so watch it."

He just tore a piece of the biscuit and put it in his mouth. He chewed slowly and she found herself watching his lips and mouth. God, he had a fine-looking mouth. There was something about it that made her wonder what it would feel like pressed against hers.

"Not bad."

"Not bad? They are damned good. Let me try your bread," she said, reached for a leftover piece of the sourdough that he'd carved out in order to make his bread bowls.

The first taste of it against her tongue made her want to moan. It was so good. She loved bread, and this loaf was everything. The texture and the taste were delicious, and she knew they'd complement his soup perfectly. Some doubts about the cheddar she'd added to her biscuits danced through her mind. The cheddar was sharp. Dang.

She glanced up at him.

"Not bad."

He gave a shout of laughter and she smiled when she heard it. "You're something else, lady."

She shook her head. She wasn't. She was just a woman determined to have the future she wanted. One away from the woman she'd been. So silly, she thought. But Gilbert Corners was her chance to be the woman she was becoming and find her place. Though he'd asked why she needed Gilbert Corners to succeed, she hadn't told him that if it didn't, she'd probably end up back home and back in a life that she didn't want. Staying in Lansdowne hadn't been an option for her. She'd always wanted out. But she'd used her time after college to carve out a path for herself. A path out of Lansdowne. And she wasn't going back.

She could easily see herself following in her mother's footsteps back there. Giving up her dreams to become a wife and mother. Not that there was anything wrong with that, except Indy was pretty sure she'd be crappy at them, and it wasn't her dream.

"Will they announce the winner soon?" she asked. The clouds were thickening around the edges of Gilbert Manor.

"Probably. The storm looks pretty fierce."

"Yeah, it does. I wasn't expecting storms like this when I moved here."

"Why *did* you come here?"

"Nola. She is a whiz at woodworking and joined my show for the last three years. We finished up in Lansdowne and the producers asked us to find another town in need of our help, and Nola suggested Gilbert Corners," she said.

"You're good friends then?"

"The best. We were college roommates and just hit it off. Again fate stepped in to help me out. Maybe you should be scared."

"Of you or of fate? Fate already gave me the finger and I told it to fuck the hell off."

He looked like he could handle anything life threw at him. Not just because of his size and the way he stood, as if it would take a bulldozer to move him. But also because of the confidence he exuded. Nothing seemed to faze him.

"That's an interesting thought. I guess surviving a car accident like yours would make me feel that way too."

He shrugged. "I hope you can take next weekend off because that's the one I'm claiming."

"That will work for me when I win. Glad you're available."

"Still confident after you tried my sourdough?"

"It takes more than a tasty morsel to rattle me."

"Does it?" he asked, leaning closer to her.

She shifted closer, her head tiping back and her eyes starting to close before she realized what she was doing. She stepped back then realized what she was doing. And stood her ground, her gaze meeting his. An electric spark seemed to arc between them, and the hair on her arms stood up. She was transfixed by the look in his eyes and the memories of watching his mouth move as he'd tried her biscuit. Kissing him was a foregone conclusion.

He was the first man she'd met since college who had distracted her. Or maybe it was because he was so closely tied to her future plans for Gilbert Corners that she wanted him. But no, she knew it was that mouth. And those broad shoulders and the tattoos that covered his body.

Conrad Gilbert was temptation incarnate, and no matter the outcome of today's cook-off, she knew that breaking the curse was no longer the reason why she was interested in him.

It was carnal. She'd never thought about lust at first sight. She'd always prided herself on liking men for their humor and their intellect, but Conrad had those as well. It wasn't like he was just a hottie; there was so much more to him. Which was a big red flag.

One of the reasons she'd left Lansdowne was that she didn't want to be her mother. The woman who had fallen head over heels in love and then stopped pursuing her own dreams.

And yes, this was a new century, and there was no reason she had to do that. But Indy knew that when she fell for a guy, she tended to start putting herself second, and she wasn't going to do that again.

Not even to break a curse.

"We're ready for you two now," Ophelia said.

Indy took a deep breath and followed Conrad out into the open in front of the judging table.

"May the best chef win," Ophelia said.

Indy realized she was holding her breath as they

waited to hear the results. The plates were taken up to the judges for tasting.

Conrad was announced the winner, and Indy wasn't exactly surprised, though she was a bit disappointed. She had a moment to herself while the eyes of the town were on them, and without thinking, she turned to him with a huge grin.

"Congratulations! I'm sure all of Gilbert Corners is excited that you'll be coming back next weekend to help with the spring renewal project."

She saw the shock on his face, knew there would be a price to pay for her boldness. He could deny it in front of everyone, and there was a moment when their eyes met and she was pretty sure he would.

"That's right. I'll be helping with the spring renewal, and then taking Ms. Belmont away to my lair."

Four

His lair.

She'd be lying if she said those words hadn't been on her mind since he'd issued them. He had been a good sport. The incoming storm had necessitated everyone leaving quickly, including Conrad, who just gave her a hard look and told her he'd be in touch.

What had she been thinking? She'd asked herself that question several times, but the answer was still the same. She'd felt backed into a corner so her impulsiveness had kicked in.

He hadn't been in touch despite saying he would be, and she wasn't entirely sure he'd show up today for the park renewal project she volunteered him for.

So she was the first one in the park with her garden gloves and weeder. If he didn't show up, she was planning to say he'd been here earlier and had to leave.

She groaned at the thought. It was like her dad always said, once a lie is started it can only be kept alive with more lies.

Ugh.

Nola was offering discounted coffee to the volunteers and, good as his word, Jeff had shown up and was directing most of them. Indy went to work on one of the beds near the train station.

She heard the sound of a motorcycle and glanced over her shoulder, relieved as Conrad Gilbert parked his bike, took off his helmet and walked toward her. She almost forgot to breathe as she took in his broad shoulders, skintight tee and the slim-fitting jeans that hugged his body like she wanted to. She was glad she had her sunglasses on, so maybe he wouldn't be aware of her checking him out as he walked toward her.

The closer he got though, she started to realize he was still ticked. She brushed off her knees as she stood up, guessing that it would be better to be standing than cowering at his feet when he got to her.

"Hello, Conrad. So nice to see you here today."

He glanced around as if just noticing the townspeople working industriously around him.

"Yeah, I bet. Were you worried I wouldn't show up?" he asked.

She told herself there was nothing sexy about his low-timbered, rough-edged voice, but that was a lie and she knew it. "Yes. Thank you for coming. I know it wasn't what we agreed but I had to do something for the townspeople."

"I swear if you mention the curse, I'm not going to be happy," he said.

He was being a bit of a jerk, and it was time to draw the line. She needed him back in town of course, but she wasn't going to allow him to bully her. "I won't. But to everyone in Gilbert Corners it's a real thing and we have to respect that."

He made a growling sound, shoved his hands through his thick hair and started to turn away, but Jeff Hamilton stopped him.

"Conrad, I wasn't sure you were going to actually come to town for this. I spoke to your cousin Dash on Friday. Thank you for coming and for suggesting that the Gilbert Trust pay for this."

She watched as Conrad talked to Jeff. She was surprised to learn that he'd arranged the money for this cleanup. The town council had simply said that funding had been found. She had tentatively hoped she'd already broken the curse in their eyes. Of course, she had lost the bet she'd made with Conrad, and she had no doubt he was going to be very demanding of whatever he asked of her.

"I'll help Indy," he said.

"Great," she said, realizing she'd been staring at the two men for too long. "I can use the help on this bed. There's a stubborn—"

"I meant with the organizing. This isn't the kind of thing I normally do," he said, gesturing to the ground and the overgrown flower beds.

"I'm glad to have your help on both parts of the project. I can show you what you need to do here. Do you have some extra gloves, Jeff?"

"Here, take mine. On second thought…you probably need some extra-large ones," he said, taking a pair from the canvas tote he carried and handing them to Conrad. Jeff waved and went back toward the main park area.

"I don't do menial labor."

She gave him a look down her nose that never failed to bring even the most recalcitrant person in line. "This is charity."

He growled again.

"You don't scare me. I need your help getting this thick weed out. I'm not strong enough and your T-shirt is broadcasting the fact that you should be."

"Should be?"

"I don't judge a book by its cover," she said.

Then turned and knelt back down on the ground digging the dirt around the stubborn root. A moment later he knelt to the ground next to her. She took a deep whiff of his cologne which had been teasing her memory since he'd left her a week ago.

"Which one?"

"Right here," she said, pointing to the spot. He worked quickly and efficiently, and for someone who'd professed not to do this kind of work, he was actually really good at it. As he worked, she couldn't help but study the thorned-branch tattoos on his arms, and in the sunlight she noticed the scars underneath.

He'd been badly injured. She'd read the newspaper report on his accident when she'd done her research, but seeing the decade-old scars affected her. She almost reached out to touch him, but pulled herself back.

It was interesting to her that he chose to emphasize his injuries with thorns. She'd never be able to wear her pain on her body. She wrapped it deeply inside where she hoped no one would ever notice it. To her, Conrad had made a brave choice.

And the more time she spent with him the more he intrigued her. He was like an attic treasure, she thought whimsically. She had no idea what she was going to uncover as she pulled him into the light.

He was essentially a stranger, and she didn't want to give him any signals other than she needed his presence to convince the town that the curse was broken.

He noticed her watching him and pushed his sunglasses up on his head. "What?"

"Not bad for your first time. If you want to start from that end, we can meet in the middle. Once we get this bed weeded, we can replant the rose bushes."

"And if I don't?"

"Do it anyway," she said with a sweet smile.

She turned away but not before she caught the edges of a slight grin on his face.

Conrad refused to admit that he was starting to enjoy himself with Indy. She was funny with her little asides and when she forgot herself, she sang little snippets of Taylor Swift songs under her breath—

which she clearly didn't know the words to because she sort of hummed half of the time.

It didn't change the fact that he was still pissed off at her for forcing him to come back to Gilbert Corners, but in her shoes, he might have done the same. And he respected that. Grudgingly but still. He respected hcr.

He pulled his phone from his pocket and noticed he'd missed a call from Dash. He got up and started to walk away.

"Hey, where are you going?"

"I have to make a call. I'll come back," he said. He wasn't used to explaining himself to anyone, and he didn't particularly like it. He moved down away from the train station and the crowds of townspeople. Some of them seemed genuine curious about him. A few stopped him to congratulate him on the success of his show.

"Con?"

"Yeah, what's up?"

"Just checking to make sure you're okay," Dash said; there was a note in his voice that Conrad hadn't heard in a long time. Something that he remembered from the teenage years before like had changed.

"Why?"

"Saw a picture on social media of you in Gilbert Corners. I'm pretty sure hell hasn't frozen over—"

"Fuck off. You know she told everyone I was coming," he said, but there was no heat in it. He was happy to hear Dash laughing. Something his cousin didn't do very often.

"I do—you just normally don't allow yourself to be manipulated like that."

"Well between her comment and you donating the funds for the project, I couldn't *not* show up."

"I thought that might be the case, but that's why I was vague about either of us showing up to help. So… Indy Belmont?"

"What about her?"

"You like her?"

"I hadn't realized I'd dialed in to your talk radio show, Dr. Dash," Conrad said.

"So that's a yes."

"I'm hanging up now and I'll mention to Jeff that you can't wait to come help next weekend."

He hung up the phone and pocketed it. The accident had changed so much between him and his cousin, but until this moment, he hadn't fully realized what it had taken from them. None of them had been the same after. Conrad had leaned into his anger as he always did and let that drive him away from Gilbert Corners and their grandfather, but also from Dash. Something he wasn't going to allow to continue.

"Would you like an iced coffee?"

He turned to see Indy standing a polite distance from him holding one of two tumblers toward him. "Figured you might want something before we start planting."

"Trying to butter me up?"

"Is it working?"

"No."

He took the tumbler from her and their fingers brushed. Her hands were cool and unblemished, he noticed, her fingers long with no nail polish. He almost turned his hand to take her fingers in his but she pulled her hand back quickly. She blushed as she tucked her hand into the back pocket of her jeans. There was something innocent about her and he didn't understand it. She was so bold most of the time.

But every time they touched, it popped up.

"So…tell me about you," he said.

She tipped her head to the side studying him. "Why do you want to know?"

"I want to be able to give the police as much information as I can on my blackmailer," he said sardonically. "It's called getting to know someone."

"Oh, you just don't strike me as someone who does small talk."

"You're making me regret asking."

She threw her head back and laughed, and a shaft of desire went through him. On the surface there was nothing about Indy Belmont that should have attracted him, yet here he was getting turned on.

"You know about my show *Hometown, Home Again* so I'm guessing you mean here in Gilbert Corners. I own the bookshop across the way as well as a Victorian house over on Maple. I thought Gilbert Corners would be a nice place to live and work for the next few years," she said.

"Is it?"

"Well, there was this curse…"

He shook his head at her. She gave him a sheepish

grin. "Sorry. I love it here. I mean my house needs more work than I expected and the foot traffic in town isn't as lively as I'd like, but I do a good business online, so I'm good. We've already filmed me making over the bookshop and Java Juice. So next up we're focusing on my Victorian house. I've been hunting for authentic pieces from that era to fill the rooms."

"And you're fixing up the town too?"

"Yes, that's what my show is about. Well, I'm trying. I mean, this town should be a weekend tourist destination and no one gets off the train here," she said. "Half the businesses on Main are closing down. I have friends who own their own businesses who I want to open shops here, but right now… I don't blame them for saying no."

He finished his iced coffee and put the tumbler on the ground. "So will you stay here after you finish fixing it all up?" He gestured to everyone working in the park.

"I don't know. What about you?" she asked.

Her answers felt…pat, like she was hiding something. Her show was successful; when he'd gone back home after the cook-off he'd watched a few episodes, getting turned on watching her work in her overalls and making molding with a table saw. Not what he would have classified as one of his turn-ons but his erection said otherwise. "What about me?"

"Why did you leave Gilbert Corners?" she asked.

He shut down. He might like her and he planned to

have her in his bed. But he never discussed his past. "That's not small talk," he said.

"Why not?" she asked in that soft, gentle way that he was coming to like a little too much. If she'd been demanding he would have walked away, but there was a genuineness to the question he wouldn't ignore.

"It's complicated," he said at last.

"Was it because of the accident? I heard your grandfather died right after you'd recovered. That would make it hard to come back here," she said.

She'd given him an acceptable reason for not wanting to be here. He could just smile and nod, but the fact was he didn't want to lie to her. "No. It's because of my grandfather himself. The old bastard made me miserable, and I want nothing to do with anything that he loved."

She stared at him for a moment than nodded. "I'm sorr—

"Let's get these rosebushes planted. Our groundskeeper used to water the ground before planting. I'll get a watering can."

He turned and walked away from her and the conversation. The last thing he wanted to discuss was his grandfather or this damned town. No matter how much Indy turned him on, he needed to finish this up and get out of town.

The sun was hot, and he heard the sound of kids laughing and playing, and all he could remember was how quiet and somber Gilbert Manor had been when he'd first arrived there.

* * *

Indy was starting to get a better picture of why the Gilberts had left Gilbert Corners. If Conrad hated his grandfather…maybe the other cousins did as well. But he was gone now and there was no reason for Conrad to stop coming here. Of course she hadn't been able to make herself go back to campus after… well, after. So she knew that a place could often hold memories that logic couldn't help her get beyond.

Except that Conrad looked like someone who didn't have those kinds of issues. Which she immediately chided herself for thinking. She knew better than to judge him based on his life. Everyone had stuff in their past that they were dealing with.

His surly attitude should be all she needed to tell her that he was dealing with something. She'd thought it stemmed from the accident, but now she wondered if the accident was just the tip of the iceberg. She told herself she wanted to help Conrad because he was tied to Gilbert Corners and the alleged curse.

But she knew that was a lie. She wanted to help him because she liked him. As surly as he could be, there was a decent man underneath. And he was hot, which shouldn't have anything to do with it, but there it was.

The first man she'd noticed as a woman in five years *would* be Conrad, wouldn't it? He was difficult but also complex. There was so much more to him that his domineering chef persona. Instead of deterring her, that made her keener to get to know him.

He came back with a watering can, and she realized she'd been watching him the entire time.

"Why didn't you dig the hole for the plant?"

"Ah, you kind of sounded like you knew what you were doing," she said.

"Here, hold this," he said, handing her the watering can.

He dug a hole and then tossed the shovel down. "Put some water in. But not too much. We don't want to drown the roots."

"You actually did more than watch your groundskeeper, didn't you?"

"Yeah. The staff were nice to me when I came to live with the old bastard."

"You shouldn't call him that."

"Why not? That's what he was," he said.

She carefully poured in the water and he gestured for her stop. Then he took the rose plant and set it into the hole he'd made.

"Can you hold it upright while I cover the roots?" Conrad asked.

"Yes. Sorry. I don't know why I said that."

He didn't say anything in response, just covered over the roots and then took the watering can and put more water on top of the soil. They planted the other three rose bushes in silence, working together as a team.

She wished she could unsay that thing about his grandfather. That was the problem with being her. She was impulsive all the time. She never thought things through, just blurted them out.

"I was trying—"

"I know you were trying to be nice because that's who you are. But I'm just as much of a bastard as he was. I can't help myself."

He leaned on the shovel and stared at her. "Sorry."

She had a feeling he didn't often apologize and didn't want to make a big deal out of it. "How about I make you some lunch as sort pax?"

"You mean before I take you away for the weekend I won," he reminded her drily.

"Yes. Want to meet me at my place? I walked over," she said.

"Sure, I'll take my bike over after I return the watering can and shovel," he said.

"I'm number 8 Maple Street."

"I'll see you there," he said.

Yikes!

Her house was still not finished; inviting Conrad over had seemed like the right thing to do, but now she was mentally going through it trying to remember if she had any unfinished projects lying around.

She pushed that to the back of her mind. She'd done some good work with the house, uncovering the herringbone wood floors which she'd sanded and then sealed. She was nervous for him to see all the work she'd put into it. For her, this house would be like letting him see her naked…more intimate than he even knew.

She went over to help Nola clean up and then thanked everyone for helping out, deliberately stalling before she walked to her house. When she got there Conrad's bike was in her driveway, but he wasn't. As she got closer, she noticed he was sitting on the Hammonds's front porch talking to Miss Martha and Miss Jean-Marie. He waved at her as she approached and said goodbye to the elderly ladies.

She fumbled with her old skeleton key to open her door and finally got it to work. She opened the door, which she had repaired when she first moved in. The foyer had terrazzo tiles on the floor and the twelve-foot ceilings created an open and cool space. She had a table next to the door where she tossed her keys into a bowl. She toed off her tennis shoes and then turned as Conrad closed the door behind himself.

"There's a bathroom through that door if you want to wash up. The kitchen is down to the left. I'm going to go use the master bath."

He didn't say anything, but she already knew he wasn't chatty. She was curious to see what he thought of her place, but also to learn more about him. He'd mentioned his grandfather, and given that local lore held that it was the *Gilbert* curse, maybe the surly old man was responsible for everyone feeling that way.

She liked Conrad, and there was something about him that she trusted. But at the same time, she sensed the danger in him.

She needed to be cautious. She didn't think he'd harm her, but she knew herself, and there was a very real risk that she'd let herself fall for him. And Conrad Gilbert wasn't the kind of man who wanted women falling for him.

She would do well to remember that. But when

she came into the kitchen and found him already assembling ingredients for their lunch, she knew it was going to be harder than she planned.

Five

Her kitchen hadn't been renovated but had a working stove top, which was all he needed. He decided he'd make her some lunch before they left. He had been rude, but that didn't bother him. He knew most people expected him to be—either because he was born with the proverbial silver spoon, or they knew that his moniker of Beast wasn't just a cute marketing one.

But he'd seen real hurt in her eyes and…

He wasn't going to delve deeper than that.

It was safe to say that Indy had horrible eating habits. He found a forgotten stick of butter in the back of a drawer, along with a block of cheddar cheese and generic store brand white bread. Her cabinets revealed no seasonings to speak of, but he found some salt and pepper packets from a local take-out place in a drawer.

"What are you doing?"

"Making lunch," he said.

"Oh well thanks. I am sorry I trapped you into coming today. I just…no excuses, sometimes my mouth just goes off without warning," she said with a grin that made him want to pull her into his arms and kiss her until they were both naked.

He looked back to the kitchen counter. She'd had an underripe tomato and some wilted lettuce in her fridge. Along with leftovers of some rotisserie chicken.

"Chicken salad or grilled cheese?"

"I don't have any mayo," she said.

"Of course you don't. What were you planning to serve me?"

"Subs from Jacob's Deli. They deliver."

He said nothing, just continued going through her pantry and fridge until he had assembled everything he thought he could use. She pulled out one of the stools, sat at the breakfast counter and watched him.

He forgot that he was in Gilbert Corners and focused only on Indy. He wanted to impress her. He admired the work she'd done on her house, and the way that she'd used her determination and kindheartedness to rally the community to make improvements. He remembered the town, and it had taken more than the money that Dash and he had allocated to get them motivated to clean up the park.

He guessed it was all down to her.

"Have you ever done that cooking show where they only give you a few ingredients?" she asked.

"No, I'm not that kind of chef."

"What kind are you?" she asked. "You don't have a restaurant, do you?"

"Not anymore."

"So you had one?" she asked.

"Yes."

"Ugh. Are you seriously going to just answer everything with one word?"

"Probably."

"The next time you do that you have to..."

"What?"

She shook her head. "So how'd you start cooking."

He pretended he didn't hear that. The last thing he wanted to do was get into postaccident Conrad. In fact, there was very little about himself he wanted to discuss. Maybe a sliver of time when he'd been eight to ten years old and life had been good.

"You said you own the bookshop?"

She tilted her head and reached over to steal a piece of cheese she'd sliced for their sandwiches. "I do. I love bookstores. I used to spend all my money at the bookstore in Lansdowne...that's where I grew up. So when I graduated and came back home to 'figure myself out' and it was up for sale, my parents suggested I buy it and run it."

"Did you?"

"Yeah. But the town was dying, so I started making YouTube videos and then invited friends to come to town and help me make over different abandoned shops. I talked Nola into coming to town and opening a bakery. Which she did. Then my parents used their contacts to talk more families into either coming back to town or enticing their kids back. And then I got my show."

"Sounds impressive. Why'd you leave?"

She chewed her lower lip for a second, drawing his eyes to her mouth. She had a full lower lip and a cute little Cupid's bow on her top lip, which he'd noticed when he'd watched her videos. He really wanted to kiss her.

"I could never tell if my success was mine or because of my parents. I have my own show, but a big part of my success was due to my parents' contacts and easy loans were used as an incentive to encourage people to move back and start businesses. Everyone in town made all of that possible."

"So you came here?" he asked. He was only half listening to her. In his mind he was exploring the softness of her mouth, but this was important to Indy and he wanted to know about her.

"Yeah. I need to prove that I can do it without them. I know how that sounds," she said with a little shrug.

"It's cool—I get it." He'd always been all about proving himself to everyone.

"What about you? How'd you become a chef instead of a CEO like your cousin Dash?" she asked.

He could do this, tell her the safe stuff. The simple answer he gave when strangers asked him. "Well I dropped out of college thanks in part to the accident. I was in a medically induced coma and then rehab for most of my junior year, so I didn't go back. I went to Europe and took dishwashing jobs to piss my grandfather off and learned to cook."

"Did you become a chef to tick him off?" she asked carefully, reaching over to steal another piece of cheese from his tray.

"Partially, but not really. I just loved it. I had a really good mentor and once I worked my way up from sous-chef to *chef de partie*, I knew that I was hooked," he said, smiling to himself as he remembered some of the kitchens he'd worked in, and the people. He'd eventually earned a Michelin star and then felt like he'd reached the pinnacle. That was when he transferred control of the kitchen to his sous-chef and started making his TV show.

He saw her put the piece of cheese in her mouth and chew it slowly. Inwardly he groaned. He needed to get laid, either with Indy or someone else. Because he felt like he was one big hormone at this point. He hadn't been this horny since he'd been a teenager.

"What about you? Is breaking curses your passion?" he asked to lighten things up.

She shook her head and her curls bounced around her face as she gave him a self-conscious look. "I'm not sure I actually broke anything."

She was still hiding something. From experience he knew that passion only came when faced with a desperate choice; only then would a person find the thing that they were called to do. For him it had been cooking. For Indy, well she didn't seem like the kind of lady who had ever had to face that choice.

Watching Conrad in the kitchen, he was starting to make more sense to her. At the park earlier today, he'd held himself as a sort of aristocrat in his fiefdom, but here in the kitchen he was different. There was a harmony to him and his movements, and she struggled to keep from staring at him.

Yeah, that was the reason why she couldn't keep her eyes off him. It had nothing to do with the skintight T-shirt and his muscly arms. The choice of thorns wrapping around his body wasn't one she understood. She wanted to ask about them. Why was she hesitating? It wasn't like he'd feel pressured to answer her.

He'd probably never done anything just to be nice, which was sort of her modus operandi. She wanted to ask him about his past and how the car crash changed him. But that would be intrusive and she wanted to be chill maybe more refrained.

"Do your tattoos have special meaning?"

"Yes."

She waited to see if he was going to elaborate, but it was clear he wasn't going to. "Thorny bushes aren't the typical tattoo, and what's that thing mean?"

She leaned forward across the counter and touched the stylized symbol on his left forearm.

"It's the Celtic symbol for brother," he said.

"Do you have a brother? I thought it was just you and your cousins."

He had finished chopping the cheese and had mashed together some herbs that she hadn't known she owned in a bowl. He reached above her head to the pot rack where she had a frying pan her grandmother had given her when Indy had left home.

"No brother. Dash and I got them together."

"He's your cousin, right?"

He gave her a sardonic look. "You know he is."

"I do. Figured I'd keep asking similar questions and see if you open up a bit."

He took the pan to the sink and washed and then put it on the burner to heat up. "I'm not going to."

He didn't talk while he made their sandwiches and she sort of just stared at his butt until she realized what she was doing. She got up and set places for both of them at the counter. "What would you like to drink?"

"I didn't see anything but milk in your fridge."

"I made sun tea. Let me go and get the pitcher."

She went outside and collected the pitcher she'd set out this morning before she'd left for the park. The sugar had melted and the tea was that perfect amber color on the cusp of turning brown. It was just the way she loved it.

She came back inside and Conrad had finished the sandwiches and somehow made a salad out of her sad looking lettuce. She filled two glasses with ice and then poured the tea over it and sat down next to him.

"So..."

He turned, arching one eyebrow at her.

"Thanks for lunch."

"No problem. I was mean to you earlier."

"You were?" she wondered when he meant. He was a brusque person and she'd had to push him back in line, but he hadn't hurt her. Not really.

"I was. Now we're square."

"Because you said so?"

"Yeah," he said, before taking a bite of his sandwich.

She turned her attention to her plate and took a taste of the grilled cheese he'd made and almost moaned out loud. It was literally the best tasting sandwich she'd ever had. How had he made this out of her crappy ingredients?

"You like it?"

She was about to gush over the sandwich but then turned to meet his gaze. "Yup."

He waited a beat and then threw his head back and laughed. He didn't say anything else while they finished their lunch, but she felt like something had changed between them. Maybe enough to just ask him to do her a favor?

She didn't think so. Not yet. But they were getting there. He might be a man of few words, but she was coming to realize that he actually said a lot with his gestures. His cooking for her was personal to him; he'd done it to apologize. Underneath the thorns he'd covered himself in was a man who…she wanted to get to know better. She hadn't thought of what would happen if she lost the wager, but it was getting closer to her paying up, and what would be like to go on a date with the Beast?.

"Would you—

"Want to—"

"Sorry," she said. "What was that?"

"Want to go for a ride on my bike?" he asked.

"For the weekend you won?"

"Nah, I'm going to come back next weekend for that since we've wasted half the day."

"That wasn't what we bargained for." But he was asking her to spend time with him, and he was hot and she liked him. She wanted to get to know him better. And he still intended to claim his weekend.

"No, but neither was me showing up in town for spring renewal. So…bike ride?"

No. Yes. Maybe. Somehow the thought of riding on his motorcycle was both exciting and scary. Also, she'd probably have to touch him, like really touch him, not just fantasize about it.

"Lady. It's a yes or no question."

She turned to face him, chewing her bottom lip trying to find the answer.

He reached up and rubbed his thumb over her bottom lip until it wasn't between her teeth. A shiver went through her, they were so close she could see the flecks of green and gold in his blue eyes. He had thick eyelashes and despite his brusque manner, he had kind eyes.

She licked her lips, swallowing hard.

He groaned. "Oh, hell."

Then he brought his mouth down on hers. He wasn't touching her anywhere except grazing his fingers under her chin and his mouth against hers.

But she felt him everywhere. The heat that she'd fantasized about when she'd watched him working at her kitchen counter spread through her. She trembled and opened her mouth to his as he deepened the kiss. His tongue brushed over hers. For a minute her body and mind were on the same page. She wanted to pull him closer. To deepen this kiss and she where it led next.

But memories started cascading through her and she was back on that sticky Georgia night. Everything inside her shut her down.

She pulled back and then tried to stand up and move away from him but knocked over her stool and she knew it was too much. Now she'd made things awkward. There was no going back from that.

Conrad sat back on his stool. He shouldn't have kissed her. He'd known that, but he hadn't been able to help himself. She stood across the kitchen, arms around her waist, watching him.

"I'm sorry I read the signals wrong. I didn't mean to make you uncomfortable."

He stayed where he was and did his best to make himself as small as he could. At six-five that wasn't easy, but he just pulled his energy back as much as he could. A flash of memory came to him, of Rory on the night of the accident running to him and Dash, her hair a mess and her dress partially torn, it was the look in her eyes that cinched it for him.

"Did someone force himself on you?" he asked.

He wanted to comfort her and do whatever he could to help her. But he wasn't always great at that.

He'd had to take care of the guy who'd done it to Rory and that had led to them leaving Gilbert Manor the way they had.

Her eyes got wider for a second and she nodded. "Yeah, I'm sorry. I shouldn't have leaned in like that. It's been forever and that reaction—my pulling away like that— was way out of line."

He pushed his chair back slowly as she kept talking; he wasn't even listening now as he was pretty sure she didn't know what she was saying. He just went over to her and leaned against the wall next to her. He was enraged that someone would have hurt her as he had been the night he'd seen Rory. "You have nothing to apologize for."

"I do. It's been years. I should be—"

"You are fine. Don't apologize."

She nodded. "It's just I'm still not sure what you want from me, and I can't kiss you—as much as I want to—if it's just from you winning me like a prize. I know I said you could have a weekend of my time…but not like this. Intimacy should be more than a lost bet."

Damn. He liked her. "I agree. I got carried away. From the moment I met you, your mouth has been driving me crazy. For our weekend I was never demanding anything sexual from you. I kind of said romantic to make you back down."

"I never back down," she said.

"I know, that's one of the things I like about you," he admitted.

"Just one?"

"I enjoyed kissing you," he said.

"I liked it too," she admitted with a shy smile. But she knew he wasn't sure what to say next.

"What were you planning for our weekend?" she asked, at last.

"Some free labor. Make you work in my test kitchen as my sous-chef, chopping onions or washing dishes."

"Wow, this is awkward—I don't do manual labor."

He knew she was throwing his words back at him and he almost smiled. "Tough. You lost and you have to pay up."

"Fair enough."

"I liked kissing you, so there's a pretty good chance if we spend more time together, I'll try it again. Should I leave?"

She chewed her lower lip again and then shook her head. "Don't leave like this."

"How about...we go back to what I asked you earlier. Go for a ride with me?"

She licked her lips and then straightened her shoulders. "Yes."

They cleaned up the kitchen and then went out to his bike and he could tell she was nervous. "You don't have to do this."

"I want to ride behind you," she said.

She blushed again and then put her hand lightly on his arm, rubbing her finger over the raised scar tissue there. His blood ran hotter and his cock stirred. He still wanted her. He couldn't believe he was hanging around Gilbert Corners.

He hadn't been able to really come back to this place until she'd challenged him to. For a moment, he wished he were a different man. But he wasn't. So fuck it. Right now he was going to take Indy on a ride. That was it.

The smell of spring was in the air and the sun shone brightly down on them, but there was still a bit of chill to the breeze that blew around them as they stood in her driveway. He noticed the tulips in full bloom around her mailbox and he remembered that his mom had planted them at their house a long time ago. He never let himself think of his parents. It was easier to keep those emotions hidden.

Indy was stirring things up that he'd ignored for a long time. He didn't like it. Conrad had come here intent on reminding her that he was in charge, but after he'd hurt her… After he'd seen himself being the Gilbert he had always been in Gilbert Corners, he'd changed his mind. This place brought out the worst in him, but it didn't have to.

He'd learned a lot about himself after the accident, and the most important thing was that he didn't want to be anything like his grandfather.

He handed her a helmet and she put it on and then he got on the bike and told her to get on behind him. The helmets had microphones in them so they could hear each other.

"Your voice is so intimate," she said.

"Yours is too," he said as she climbed on behind him. She put one hand in the center of his back as she settled herself on the saddle.

He turned on the bike, nudge the kickstand with his foot. He felt her hands on his waist, just lightly holding him, and his cock stirred. But she wasn't pressed against his back. Her body trembled.

"Have you been on a motorcycle before?"

"No. I've always been a scared of them."

"You don't have to do this."

"I have to do it for me."

He turned the bike and drove down Maple, away from town to the winding circular road that would lead them from the past. He didn't want to go toward the manor and his memories there. He wanted this afternoon in the sunshine, with Indy holding carefully on to him and keeping the space she needed to feel safe, to be for them.

He hadn't realized it, but once he'd seen her fear, he'd forgotten his own. There wasn't room to deal with the ghosts of his past or the anger that still dogged him. He wanted to soothe her and show her that she had nothing to worry about while she was with him.

The road was winding and as he accelerated into the turn, he felt her hands soften and then she scooted closer, wrapping her arms tightly around him as he powered out of the turn. Her touch affected him as it always did, setting fire to him like a Scotch bonnet pepper, and he knew that he wouldn't be able to resist her much longer. But he kept it cool, focusing on making this afternoon about her needs. He wanted this adventure for her, as he had a feeling that she limited her adventures to the ones she found between the pages of her books.

They rode for forty-five minutes before he pulled to a stop at the side of the road. Near the outer edges of the land that he and his cousins owned. There was a small brook not too far from here. He wasn't sure why he remembered it now, but he thought that Indy would like it.

Six

Indy hadn't expected to like the bike ride, but something had changed in Conrad once he'd cooked for her. He had seemed to understand that she'd needed some quiet, and the wind blowing past them as he'd driven them along the curving road nearby Gilbert Corners had soothed her.

Her legs were still vibrating from being on the bike when he'd stopped it and gotten off. He'd offered her his hand and now that she stood next to him, she felt awkward again.

He took off his helmet and she did the same. "That fence borders the Gilbert property."

"Y'all sure own a lot of land," she said.

"The trust does now," he said.

"Isn't that you?" she asked, as he offered her his

hand again to cross the water to the other side. They made their way up an incline that wasn't too steep.

"Dash and I provide oversight, but we don't run it," he said.

"Is it a charitable trust?" she asked. "I was surprised when we got the offer to fund the park restoration."

"Were you?" he teased. "I was pretty sure if we didn't act first, you'd be at the offices making a deal."

She smiled at that. "I hadn't thought of it, to be honest. But I have been busy trying to figure out how to break the curse."

He shook his head. "The people in this town need to stop talking about that."

She agreed; curses weren't something that most people talked about. But she could see where they'd think that the Gilbert family and the town that had been named after them might be. "Seems your family had a string of bad luck."

"Yeah," he said.

That was it. He concentrated on the path which was muddy after the spring rains but soon he found whatever he was looking for and led her through some overgrown trees and bushes. He stopped, his broad back and shoulders all she could see, and it wasn't a bad view.

Somehow riding behind him and being more in control of their touching had relaxed something inside her. And of course, Conrad just being so chill about everything, and him accepting her fears in a way she'd never been able to before had helped more than she'd expected.

From where they stood, she saw the flowers blooming in the manicured gardens near where they'd had their cook-off. The octagonal tower with its cupola was visible. It was hard for her to imagine what it had been like to grow up in a mansion.

"This is it. The best view in Gilbert Corners."

She totally agreed, she thought, staring at the way his jeans hugged his butt and then moving her gaze up to the strength of his shoulders. Everything about Conrad was honed to perfection.

He stepped aside and held his hand out to her, drawing her forward to the edge. She caught her breath. Beyond the rolling green lawn of Gilbert Manor she saw the river snaking toward the town, and from here Gilbert Corners didn't look cursed or run-down. The buildings with their Victorian turrets and spires looked picturesque.

"I guess you don't hate everything about the town."

He put his arm on her shoulder and leaned down close so that his head was level with hers. She glanced over at him.

"Tell anyone and I'll deny it."

She laughed. He sounded so surly and annoyed. And she knew that a part of him meant it.

"You dare laugh at the Beast?" he asked with a mock growl.

"If you were really a beast, I doubt I would be

laughing, but the truth is, you aren't. I think… I think you hated Lance Gilbert, not Gilbert Corners."

"Still hate, not past tense," he said.

"Why? He's dead," she said, trying to understand where Conrad was coming from. But then, she had only one person she felt anger and hatred toward, and it wasn't a close family member. Would she have found it hard to let go of her anger as well?

"I never got to have it out with him. Never had my say as an adult. We fought the night of the accident. After I punched that punk—Declan Owen attacked Rory and I broke his nose—grandfather lit into me. I was so angry I went for him, but Dash pulled me away…and we left."

She turned and put her hand on his thick biceps. Feeling this strength in him while hearing his vulnerability. She'd always believed that anger was just the prickly part of a person. The thorns they used to keep everyone at bay, and with Conrad it seemed especially true.

"Did he die before you'd recovered?" she asked carefully.

"Grandfather? No, just before I'd wised up and matured," Conrad said.

"It's hard to think of you as immature."

"Lady, you should have seen me when I was good-looking. I was all ego and confidence. I mean, I thought the world revolved around me."

"You are still good-looking," she said.

"Don't let the stubble and tattoos fool you. This body has some mileage on it."

She shook her head. "That's okay—this one does too. You just can't see it on the outside."

"Damn. Here you go reminding me I still let my ego take the lead."

"We all do. Look at me challenging you and then making a side dare," she said because things were getting too intimate. She was starting to remember how good the first moment of that kiss in her kitchen had been. And that was dangerous.

"That's because you have some big balls, lady."

She blushed but laughed. "I don't, but I like to act like I do."

He smiled down at her. "What else have you promised that you're not sure you can deliver?"

She shook her head. "I'm always sure I'll deliver—I'm just not sure how. I mean, I'm trying to organize the Main Street retailers to put on the spring fling, though I'm really a shy person."

"Your TV show would beg to differ," he said.

"That's different because it's a few close friends and a camera. So not really the entire town. But I need them to work with me."

"So you just power through until you get the results you want?"

She thought about it for a moment, realizing that she had always been like that. "I'm not six-five with a ferocious nickname. Sometimes…well, all the time, I just keep faking it, and usually people believe that I can do all the things I say."

"Even you?"

She chewed her lower lip and noticed his gaze

dropped to her mouth and then moved over to the horizon.

"Not all the time, but most of the time."

Conrad was holding on to his control with more strength than he realized he had. He couldn't put his finger on what it was about Indy that shook him and made him want her so badly. The ride hadn't done anything but sharpen his desire for her. But it was the hint of her vulnerability and that feisty spirit that made him want more than just her body.

He'd never needed anyone in his life. He'd made it a practice to keep everyone at arm's length and she should be no different. Given her ties to Gilbert Corners, she should be someone who sent him running in the opposite direction. Instead he had his arm around her shoulder trying to pretend she was just a buddy he was hanging with—except that he didn't have friends like that. He never touched anyone except for casual sex, and that didn't last as long as this.

Since the night he'd punched Rory's attacker, angering Declan enough that he'd chased them down the icy road and caused the car accident, Conrad had kept his hands to himself. The accident had helped. The first few months he hadn't been able to really use his arms and his strength had gone. But as he'd built it back, he'd made a promise to himself to keep his anger in check.

Like Indy with her confidence.

"I do that, too," he said.

"Liar. You don't have to fake confidence."

"No. I have to fake anger. It gives me a buffer and keeps people from actually making me mad."

She turned her head, and he noticed how big her brown eyes were up close. She had thick black lashes and a small birthmark under her left eye. She'd looked so prim and untouchable when he'd first met her that it had been hard for him to see the scars she'd mentioned. But they were there.

Hell, he knew that from dealing with Dash. His cousin had walked away from the car accident scot-free but dealt with more trauma than Conrad did on a daily basis.

"Why do you have to be angry?" she asked. "I didn't get anger the first time I met you."

"You didn't?"

"I mean, you were definitely trying to intimidate me, but you weren't like a bully," she said.

"I'll have to remember that for the future."

She shook her head and a strand of hair that had come free brushed against his arm. It was soft and springy, a light touch, just like Indy herself.

"Why anger?" she asked again.

He wasn't sure he wanted to get that honest with her but at the same time sort of wanted to. "It's easier. When I'm like this, people ask questions."

"Like I'm doing right now. Sorry about that," she said. "You just make me all mixed-up inside. I mean I know I shouldn't be talking so much yet I can't help it."

She took a breath and he knew she was going to keep talking. She was so close, and that botched kiss in her kitchen hadn't satisfied his yearning for her. He leaned in, slowly giving her time to pull away, and took his arm from her shoulders so she wouldn't feel trapped by him at all.

He tried to make himself stop. Told himself if she looked scared, he wouldn't kiss her, but then her eyes closed and he knew he wasn't stopping. Damn his soul, he'd trade anything for just one taste of her. One kiss that ended like an embrace should. He wanted that. Not just for her, but for himself.

"I'm going to kiss you," he said.

"I know," she retorted. "I want you to."

Her words tore through the last of his resistance. He leaned in and this time his mouth brushed hers. Knowing her fear this time, he just stayed there for a second and then her lips parted and he felt her tongue on his. Sliding into his mouth lightly. Like everything about Indy, she moved with a quickness and surety that he wondered if she was allowing her passion to override her doubts.

He opened his eyes and noticed hers were still lightly closed; he angled his head to deepen the kiss because she tasted so good. Addictive. Like the first time he'd cooked a meal that had made him famous. He felt her hands brush against his stomach, then slowly move to his sides. She didn't pull him closer and he kept the space between them, though her fingers were still on him.

He lifted his head. Her lips were moist from his kiss, slightly swollen, and her eyelids fluttered open.

She watched him for a long moment. Then sort of nodded, more to herself than to him.

"That wasn't what I expected," she said.

"Me either," he replied. He realized that if he didn't move and leave this spot right now, he was going to be tempted to kiss her again and again until they were both nude. And that felt like it might be more than she wanted. He needed specifics from her, but this wasn't the time for that.

And that wasn't why he'd come to Gilbert Corners. It wasn't why he'd brought her, which also had nothing to do with his reasons for being in GC. But he'd needed to somehow help her past that fear. Kissing Indy had been the only thing he could do after he'd brought her here to the one spot in this area where he'd always felt comfortable.

Up here, it had never mattered if he'd been an ass because he was too rich, too spoiled, too good-looking to realize that he wasn't better than everyone else. Up here, he was enough in his grandfather's eyes. Up here, his parents were still proud of him.

Now he had a new thought for this spot he hadn't visited in over ten years. Up here, Indy thought he was a better version of himself than he'd ever been.

"Ready to go back?"

No.

"Yes, I think so." That was the safe answer. And right now when she was feeling all this chaotic nervous energy, that was the only thing she could do. "Thanks for bringing me."

He didn't say anything, just extended his hand to her as they walked back down the incline toward his bike. They got there and he handed her a helmet, but before she put it on, she said, "That view up there. The way Gilbert Corners looks perfect. I want people to have that feeling when they are in town."

He shook his head. "Perfection isn't what you are looking for."

"Well graffiti sure isn't it either," she said.

"I know. Some happy medium. I like your shop and I like the coffee place, but there are too many abandoned buildings on Main Street. I guess that's why you're filming your show here."

He had a point. She'd been reaching out to businesses, but the uptick had been slow. She knew once she started getting some more of the buildings renovated, she would entice more retailers to town. She wanted Gilbert Corners to match the image in her head. The one she'd create with her television show and her own imagination.

She smiled at him because he watched her with that intense gaze of his. "Now I don't want to sound like everyone on the town council, but I think that's down to the curse."

"Too late—you sound like 'em. But I know what you mean. Dash and I shouldn't have turned our backs on the town," Conrad said.

"Does that mean you're going to move back here?"

He shook his head. "No. But the trust can do more, and they will. Maybe we can get some more shops open on Main Street and offer incentives for remote professionals to settle in town."

Of course. Despite what he'd said when he'd showed her the town from his favorite vantage point, Conrad didn't want to be part of the town. It wasn't something she understood, but maybe as she got to know him better, she would.

"I think I can help with that when you are ready. I have a lot of contacts from the revitalization we did in Lansdowne."

"I'll make sure to let Dash know."

They drove back to town and he pulled up in her driveway. Once she was off the bike, he nodded toward her and then backed up and drove off.

She knew it was for the best. She hadn't really planned on anything that happened today. She felt exhausted from all the emotions that had been roiling through her from the moment he'd shown up at the park and helped her replant those roses.

Conrad wasn't what she'd expected yet at the same time…he was what she wanted. She shook her head and went inside to call Nola and ask if she could chat.

"Is it a cookies and ice cream chat or a tequila chat?" Nola asked.

"Both?" she said.

"Give me ten minutes and I'll be there," Nola said.

Fifteen minutes later they were both seated on the front porch in the Kennedy Rockers that Indy had restored over the holiday season. They both had a bowl of Chunky Monkey ice cream, and an opened package of Milano cookies was on the table between them.

"So, um, Conrad Gilbert."

"Yeah. I saw you two working together. What happened? It was pretty busy at the coffee shop so I couldn't really tell what was happening with you guys."

She didn't hesitate to tell Nola everything. This woman was like a soul sister. From the moment they'd met they both sort of got each other.

"He left just like that?" Nola asked after Indy finished.

"Yeah. I mean I didn't ask him to stay. I don't know that I wanted him to stay," she said, taking a big spoon of ice cream, hoping that it would numb her mouth and maybe give her brain freeze so she could think of anything other than how it had felt to kiss him or to hold on to his back as they'd ridden on his bike the way his back had felt pressed against her chest. Her breasts felt fuller when she remembered that adn she hadn't washed her shirt when she got home because the scent of his aftershave lingered on it.

"Maybe he knew that and that's why he left," Nola said. "But he's usually all growly on this TV show. But he's different in person. Not like he used to be, but not like he is on TV either."

"I mean sort of, but it's more of a bluff, I think. But there is a part of him that's almost sweet."

"He sounds like a decent guy which makes sense because Dash is super nice too. I heard old Lance was a piece of work but that was from the factory workers who he fired. So who knows?"

"Maybe. How did Conrad and his cousins end up here?" she asked Nola, because if Lance wasn't a great person, then where did that innate kindness come from?

"I can't really remember the details because I was a kid, but Conrad's and Dash's parents were killed in a plane crash. They were brought here to live at Gilbert Manor. They went to our school for like two weeks. I was in third grade and they were in fifth. That's all I know. Rory was in my class. She was so shy but very sweet."

Indy looked over at her friend, wishing she knew more of the story. She was trying to imagine what it had been like to lose his parents like that. She thought about what he said about not being able to talk to his grandfather as an adult. What if it wasn't just his grandfather he wanted to talk to, but also his parents?

"Did you go to that party the night of the accident?" she asked.

"Yes, it was something else. Declan Owen, whose family did business with the Gilberts, was drunk and hitting on Rory, and then something happened and Conrad knocked him out. Lance told Conrad and Dash that he should disown his grandchildren for causing a scene. Conrad went after the old man and Dash pulled him off and said something, I wasn't close enough to hear, but my mom said it was heated. Then they drove off, going too fast. Declan went after them. We all heard the crash."

"Where did it happen?"

"Right on the bridge over the river in the middle of town. The roads were okay, but the bridge had iced over and they skidded across it. The car rolled several times. It was horrible."

Indy's heart was racing just from imagining what it had been like for Conrad in that car. He'd told her the aftermath, but now she thought she understood him a little bit better. And the man who'd been so kind to her that afternoon. Maybe he was trying to treat her the way he'd never been treated.

Seven

At midnight her phone dinged with a text message. She only had two chapters left to finish in the book she was reading and really didn't want to stop, but glanced at her phone in case it was her parents with an emergency.

Instead it was an unknown number with a New York City area code.

Intrigued, she pulled the phone closer.

UNKNOWN NUMBER: It's Con. Couldn't sleep thinking about you.

She read the message, and then reread it. How was she meant to respond? Had he texted her by mistake? To be honest, it was only the fact that Nola had come over that had allowed her to stop thinking about him. The book had provided a distraction… but to be fair, the hero had taken on Conrad's large frame, scarred face and soft lips.

Indy Belmont: It's Indy, you know that right?

UNKNOWN NUMBER: Yes.

Indy Belmont: Oh, good. Me too. Sorry things got awkward.

She saw the little dots that signaled he was typing and quickly saved his contact information in her phone.

Conrad Gilbert: It was me as much as you. GC makes my skin feel too tight. But I'm finding it hard to think of not coming back there to see you.

Indy Belmont: I wish… I wish I were different.

She dog-eared the page she was on in her book and set it aside, turning on her side to get more comfortable on her bed. Then her phone rang with a video call from Conrad. She hesitated for a second before answering it. She saw what she looked like in the camera and lifted her arm to try to make it a better angle.

But then he could see she wore her Ravenclaw nightshirt. Her hair was down and though it wasn't morning Medusa out-of-control it was a bit frizzy. She was just…well her. If he was still interested after seeing her like this…she'd be surprised.

"Hey. Just figured it'd be nicer to chat. You in bed?"

"Yeah. I am. Give me a minute to…" Whatever she was about to say, it was going to sound ridiculous. So she put the phone down and ran to the other room to get the phone holder she used when she talked to her mom and dad once a week.

She came back in time to see Conrad's camera pointing at the floor as he walked through a long hallway. She set up her phone and then tried to look alluring or sexy, but let's face it, with this nightshirt and hair…it wasn't happening.

He stopped walking and brought the camera back to his face. "I just got home."

It was really none of her business what he'd been doing, but… "What were you doing?"

"Like I said, lady, I couldn't stop thinking about you, so I was in the test kitchen."

"You were cooking?"

He shrugged as he plopped down on something. Then he reached over and clicked on a light and she realized he was in a bedroom. His?

"It's what I do when I start feeling restless," he said.

"I read. A good book sweeps me away from my own thoughts," she said. "Did you cook it all out?"

"I didn't. I wish you were here with me."

She did too. But she wondered if she'd feel the same way if he were in the same room with her. It was one thing to fantasize about being intimate with him, but she had no idea how she'd really react. The kiss outside this afternoon had shaken her to her core, made her hungry for him in a way that she hadn't thought she'd ever be able to feel again.

"Too much?"

She shook her head. "I'm just not sure about the reality of it—I mean you live in the city and I live in a place you hate."

"Ah, I thought you meant who'd be on top," he said.

Immediately her mind went to what that would be like. Her on his lap, his hands on her body, her hands on shoulders or maybe his chest.

"Con. I'm not sure this is a good idea."

He sighed. "What would be a good idea."

"I'm not sure. I do owe you a weekend, right? We need to talk about that."

"What if I call it off and we date."

"Date?"

"It's this thing where two people who like each other meet up—"

"Ha. I know what a date is—I meant it more as surprised. You don't strike me as a dating kind of guy."

"What kind of guy do I strike you as?" he asked.

"The hooking up for a hot night kind," she said.

"Well okay, I can be that if you want."

"No. I want you…" she trailed off, trying to think of what she wanted from him. *Everything.* But at the same time, she wasn't sure how that would work or if she'd even be able to be intimate with him.

He gave her a rakish smile. "I want you too, but I suspect that's not what you meant."

"It is," she said. "I just don't know."

"You want intimacy," he said.

"I do. I'm pretty sure you don't," she said.

"I called you at midnight, lady. Fuck, that seems intimate to me."

"Sorry. It's easier for me to deflect than admit what I want from you."

"I know," he said. "So about my weekend."

"With me cutting veggies in your kitchen?"

"Or something else."

"Like what?"

He thought it over for a few minutes. "You could come to the city and I'll show you around my neighborhood and then I'll cook you dinner."

"Okay. I can take the train in," she said.

"I can send a car for you."

"No thanks. Where do you live?"

"On Bleecker in an old brownstone mansion that was my parents'. It takes up half the block." He hesitated, a wistful note in his voice. "I'm lucky it stayed in my mother's family. I'll text you the address."

"Nola told me that your parents were killed in a plane crash. That sounded so awful."

"Nola Weston?"

"Yes. Do you remember her from school?" she asked him. This weekend agreement was dangerous because he was making her think of him in a way that was safe. It was okay to kiss him and let him dominate her dreams, but in reality, she knew he'd dominate her life. And she was on her way to something bigger.

"Not really, but she was friends with Rory," he said. "I don't have any friends in Gilbert Corners."

"You do now," she said.

"You?"

"Unless you don't like me."

"I'm calling you at midnight… I think I like you."

She wrinkled her nose at him. "Sounds like you're not sure."

"Lady, if you were here with me, you'd know how much I *like* you."

There was a note of raw desire in his voice that sent heat down her entire body, her breasts felt fuller and her niples hardened. She shifted her legs under the sheets and wished she and Conrad were in the same room. She had enjoyed kissing him. He'd stirred to life desires that she'd told herself she didn't miss, and until this moment she'd almost believed that lie.

But there was no way she could deny that she wanted Conrad.

He wasn't a man used to denying himself when he wanted a woman, but Indy was different. She'd shown him her sass and determination. Honestly, if he'd been able to forget about her, he would have been…well not happier per se but it would have made life easier. Instead he was catching feelings for her. She'd been in his head and on his palate all night.

He'd showered and masturbated when he got

home, hoping that would level off his hormones and give him a modicum of relief, but again, no. Indy Belmont was still in his blood and playing hell with his senses. Nothing he'd created in the kitchen had satisfied him either.

Probably because he had only seen the glimpse of the woman she was. She'd shown him the spunky, feisty bookshop owner determined to rejuvenate her town. She'd given him a taste of her passion when she'd touched him and kissed him in her kitchen.

He admired her. He wasn't going to deny it. But he needed her naked in his bed. On top of him and under him, facing him, her back pressed against him. He wanted her every way he could have her. He just felt like if he had her then maybe, he could finish that dish which danced elusively around him. And then, maybe, he could stop thinking about her.

She shifted on the bed. He could tell she was wearing some sort of T-shirt. Her hair was down—not as long as he'd guessed it was—and it was curlier. It framed her face and fell only to her shoulders. She had on a pair of horn-rimmed glasses and her heart-shaped face was free of makeup.

Her lips were a natural dusky rose color, and her eyes were big and brown behind the lenses of her glasses, inviting him closer to delve into her secrets. Or was that only his imagination? He wanted her in a way that he hadn't wanted a woman in a long time.

She hadn't responded after he had emphasized how much he liked her. Hell, he had a hard-on and they hadn't been doing anything but talking.

Except talking was all it seemed to take sometimes. Her voice was soft and gentle late at night. Though he knew she lived alone, it seemed she had quieted her voice.

"Did I scare you off?" he asked. Because he didn't figure her for a woman who'd be scared of anything. Especially a man.

"No. I wish I could be some kind of sophisticated woman who knew what to say to that. But I'm not."

"Just be yourself. Did I scare you?"

"No," she said, shaking her head making a few tendrils of her curls bounce around her face.

"Turn you on?"

She chewed her lower lip for a minute and then slowly nodded.

"Good. That's what I was hoping for. You turn me on too."

"Really?" she asked sounding skeptical.

"I'm not a guy to lie."

"Oh, I got that about you," she said. "You have all these upper-crust manners some of the time, but most of the time you walk around as if you own the world."

"Don't I?" he asked, teasing her.

She shook her head. "No, dear beast, you don't."

Dear beast.

He had felt like one ever since that night ten years ago. Not the car accident but who he'd been before it. The way he'd turned away women who he'd deemed not pretty enough for him, hurting more than one according to overheard comments later in the evening.

Then he'd beaten that punk after he'd attacked Rory. Screamed at his grandfather.

But he'd never felt at home with the name. He'd wore it because he'd known deep in his soul that there was something savage about him. Even with his money and manners, there had been something monstrous about him since the moment his parents had died.

"If I did, would it be easier to claim you?" he asked her.

She laughed, and it was a loud full-bodied sound that made his dick even harder. "I've given you the wrong impression of me if you think there is anything easy about me."

He smiled but it was getting harder to keep things light. No, there was nothing easy about Indy. She was complex and intricate. A nice person but not a pushover. Sexy and shy. She was so many differing things at the same time, and all it did was heighten his need to claim her as his own.

"I remember you bullying me into coming to the spring renewal even though I won."

"Bullying!"

"You weren't about to take no for an answer."

"You're right about that. But I just pushed because you're big enough to take it."

"I am big enough," he said, the words coming unbidden. They were his truest desire in this moment. His voice had even dropped a level and sounded husky to his own ears.

"Is that what you want?" she asked, her own voice slightly trembling.

"More than anything," he admitted. He had no problem with honesty. His problems lay with other things like commitment.

"Why?" she asked. "I googled you earlier. You date some really hot women."

"I don't date," he said. Knowing that he could say he just fucked them. She wouldn't understand it. He was different with her. Actually, he was different because of her, he realized.

"Then what is this about?"

"I thought it was about winning a bet," he said.

She tipped her head to the side, eyeing him for a long minute, and he let her. He had no illusions about the man he was. He might not like all the parts of himself, but he knew ever since he'd woken up in the hospital that he'd tried to be better. To do better. He was never going to be anyone's idea of a white knight. He didn't want to be. He just wanted to be the best of who he was.

Ofttimes that was a beast.

Today...he'd seen someone else when he'd taken her for a ride on his bike. He'd seen a man that he didn't know and wasn't sure he wanted to. But with her, that man was lurking in his skin.

She wanted to ask him more about why he didn't date but wasn't sure that she was ready for the answers. She wanted him, and that was enough to deal with on its own but she also really liked him. A part of her wished she could write him off as a spoiled asshole. He owned that about himself, and that had made her like him even though it shouldn't have.

There were massively overgrown vines around him, blocking her view of who he truly was. But every once in a while, she caught a glimpse of someone who made her heartbeat faster, and not just with lust.

"So did I scare you off?" he asked. His voice had a low graveled whiskey tone that made every sense of her body take notice.

The sheets on her legs felt too heavy and the shirt against her body to thick. She wished for the courage to be naked with him. To find her way into his arms and this time really experience everything he had to give her.

It made her uncomfortable to admit it, even just to herself, but Conrad was the embodiment of everything she'd ever wanted in a man. He was driven and successful, a man who commanded respect. He was blunt and asked for what he wanted in a way that made her feel almost superficial in her other interactions with people.

"Lady?"

"Yes?"

"The way you keep licking your lips makes me want to feel your tongue on my skin…" he said, his voice getting even deeper. "Did that scare you?"

"No," she said slowly as a moist heat pooled between her legs. She hadn't wanted like this in way too long.

"What are you thinking about?" he asked.

"What it would feel like to lick your chest and then work my way lower," she said.

"Damn. That's..."

"Too much?"

"Not at all. Honestly, I like it."

"I do too," she said.

"I should let you go," he said after a few moments had passed.

"Yes. I have to open the shop in the morning and then my assistant will be in around noon. So I could come see you after that—does that work?" she asked.

"I forgot..." he trailed off.

She arched both eyebrows at him, angling her head to the side. "That I have a life and don't just exist when you want to see me?"

"Indy, you cut me. I just meant I forgot what it was like to run a business. Why don't we do it next weekend?"

"Do you work during the week?"

"I pretty much work in the test kitchen when we aren't filming, developing new menus for the restaurant, but I'm ahead of the game there," he said.

She rolled on her side, starting to get sleepy but reluctant to end the call. It had been a long time—maybe forever—since she'd wanted to just keep talking to someone like this. "How do you develop a menu? I'm not even sure I know what that means."

"Well," he said, punching the pillow behind his head and sinking down onto it. "I start with seasonal ingredients and then see what they inspire. Right now we're working on the spring menu for the restaurant. So I call our suppliers and see what they are going to have—some years the crops vary—and then I talk to my partner and the head chef at the restaurant and we work together to come up with dishes."

"I never realized that cooking was so creative," she said, her words sleepy. "I'm never going to be able to beat you in a cooking contest."

"No, you're not," he confirmed. "I think I'm putting you to sleep."

"You're not. It's late and I had an exhausting day." It had started with the surprise of Conrad at the cleanup, then their kiss and the bike ride. Nola's revelations and then his call. Her mind was too tired to process everything and she knew she needed sleep. But she didn't want him to go.

"I'll let you go and get some sleep."

She smiled at him, touching her phone screen where his mouth was. She remembered the feel of his lips on hers making her mouth tingle. "I'm so glad you called me."

He looked down at her and gave her that devilish grin of his that sent heat through her entire body.

"I'm glad I did too."

"Good night, lady," he said in that low voice that was straight out of her hottest dreams.

"Good night, dear beast." She realized that no matter how ill-advised it was, she was starting to fall for him.

He disconnected the call and she rolled over on the bed, throwing her arms wide, staring at the ceiling. She liked him. Like really liked him. And he wasn't at all someone she should. He hated this town. And she'd fallen in love with this place the moment she'd seen it. The buildings were solid just neglected and needed some care and new life to them. This place had made her feel like she'd found home.

Gilbert Corners was her future. It felt like there was no place for the two of them to meet except for the contest, and, well, in lust. Maybe that was what she needed. Actually, she *knew* it was. She needed him to help her get past her lingering fears and finally give into to the desires that thinking about Conrad stirred in her.

And that was enough.

That was more than enough, she thought.

Eight

Conrad looked up from his morning coffee as the doorbell rang at his home in New York City. A few moments later, Dash came into the kitchen.

"Morning."

"Morning," Conrad said as he watched his cousin make himself a cup of coffee before sitting down across from him. Dash took a section of the newspaper that Conrad always had delivered and started reading it.

"Am I supposed to ask why you're here?" Conrad asked after a few more minutes had passed.

Dash didn't answer but put the newspaper down. "No. Can we pretend that this is normal?"

"No."

"Rory's doctor is retiring," Dash said, drumming his fingers on the table.

"You said."

"Well I tried to influence the board to hire a specialist I found who I think might actually help her come out of the coma, but they weren't receptive."

"Can't you move her to wherever the specialist is?"

"He's in Sweden, so it's not ideal for me to continue to see her," Dash said. "And he won't come just to be Rory's doctor."

"Want me to try to convince them?" Conrad asked, putting his own paper down and sitting up taller.

"No. That would just make things worse. Apparently, Gilbert Corners General Hospital which owns and runs GC Care Home doesn't want a Gilbert throwing his weight around."

"They said that to you? I mean, the trust pretty much keeps that place running."

"Which I also pointed out," he said. "That didn't win me any points with them. The board told me they'd let me know when a replacement had been found."

"Fucking hell," Conrad said.

"I know. It's almost ten years that she's been in that damned coma. I don't know what to do. Should I move her? I could probably donate a wing or something at a private hospital."

Dash was looking for solutions, and to be honest, Con knew he didn't have one. He thought about Gilbert Corners and what he'd seen yesterday. "I wonder if you don't take one of the older buildings that's run down in the town and make it into a private facility. Hire your expert to come and work there. Kind of give him carte blanche to set it up."

Dash leaned back, stretching his arm along the back of his chair and looking out the window to the manicured garden. Conrad left his cousin to his thoughts, but the idea made him think a little bit more of what Indy wanted to see in the town. Conrad could open a test kitchen and offer cooking classes. Maybe in part of the old factory. But that wasn't going to help Gilbert Corners. Was he just thinking about himself again? He needed to think bigger and bring in more business.

But did he really want to get more involved?

"Yeah, you know, I like that idea. Thanks, Con."

"No problem. What do you think of me taking over part of the old factory?" he asked.

"And doing what?"

"Maybe put in a test kitchen where I could teach locals to cook, or I could get in touch with some friends I know who have established schools. Just use part of it. Is that dumb?"

Dash shook his head. "I like it. I'll look into it. Your name will probably draw some people from surrounding areas. But you'd have to be in GC. And we both know how much you hate that. Right?"

He shrugged. It was complicated. There was a lot of space. He could put in a filming studio and shoot in GC. Also, his former business partner was always needling him to open another restaurant. Would moving back there be a good thing for him? He'd be in the shadow of Gilbert Manor and memories of his overbearing grandfather which never brought out the best in Conrad. "I don't know."

Dash put his hands on the table and leaned forward. "I'm not going to say no to you, but if you start something and then abandon it, you'll be no better than Grandfather when he closed that factory. We can't go in big and start building stuff only to leave."

"I get it. I wouldn't do that," Conrad said, but he knew there was still a chance he might. Maybe Dash was right.

He shoved his hands through his hair and then sat back. "So it has to be something that doesn't require my name. Let me talk to the television network. Maybe we could partner and use it as off-site place to nurture young talent and rotate different celebrity chefs through a new TV series."

"That's a good start. I think you were right about the town needing our attention, and this is the kind of project that would help the locals. I hate to admit this, but I sort of always lumped the town and Grandfather together."

Conrad had, too, and it had taken Indy to make him realize that the townspeople were actually decent and nothing like his grandfather. "I agree. It's time we made it up to them."

"Never heard you talk like this."

"Honestly, never thought I would. But I met someone recently who is making me see things differently."

"The bookshop girl?"

"She's a woman," Conrad said. Except Indy was so much more than just a woman. She was a temptress, so sweet and sexy making him hunger for her.

"Is she? Want to tell me about her?"

"No," he said. He wanted to keep Indy to himself but then he realized that he did want to talk about her. Maybe Dash would hear something or see something in his comments that would allow Indy make sense to him.

So he told Dash about her. He didn't leave out anything because they were close and had no secrets. They both saw each other for who they were. Conrad might be the Beast and Dash the Prince Charming of the Gilbert family, but they were the same inside.

Deeply protective, defensive, and not afraid to walk away from everything. That bond had been forged at their parents' deaths and hadn't been tarnished through the accident that had shaped their destiny.

Conrad talked through lunch, and they grabbed beers to sit by the pool when he'd finally wound down.

"I like the sound of her. She's not your usual type," Dash said.

"No shit. That's the problem," Con said. "Or am I missing something?"

"Only time will tell. You should think of a relationship with her the same way you do about opening that kitchen in Gilbert Corners. Only do it if you're going to see it through. Otherwise, you'll both end up getting hurt."

* * *

The bookshop was busy on Sundays as a rule. Nola set up a pop-up coffee stand in the front of the shop and Indy hosted a children's reading hour between two and three so that parents could browse in her shop or other stores on Main Street.

She'd dreamt of Conrad all night and woken up hungry for him. She couldn't wait for the weekend. It felt like she'd spent most of her adult life waiting for something, and until yesterday, she hadn't realized what it was. She'd frozen a part of herself, afraid she wouldn't find her own path after that horrible date and the attack that had followed. Even Wayne hadn't really been able to handle it.

He'd been her high school boyfriend, and when she'd come back home, she'd tried to date him again. He was safe and he loved her. But she'd never been able to relax with him. She told herself she left her hometown because he got engaged, but she knew it was really to spare herself any residual disappointment.

She knew she'd been lucky to escape with just some scrapes, bruises and a fear of intimacy. She'd punched her attacker Ben so hard in the throat that he hadn't been able to speak for a few weeks. The claw marks on his eyes had taken longer to fade.

The incident had made Indy face the violence within herself, and whenever she saw Ben on campus, she'd felt sickened being near him and an irrational sense of pride at the damage she'd caused him. Eventually she dropped out and started going to online school.

That incident had cemented in her that she had a very large capacity for doing violence to another person. She knew if pushed, she'd react that way. And until last night, she hadn't realized that she also had a lot of passion inside her. She'd shied away from anything that stirred her emotions, wrapped herself in a bubble and faked a friendliness that wasn't true to herself.

But even Wayne, who she'd always trusted, hadn't been able to break through the wall she'd built around herself. They'd worked together on remodeling the bookshop in town and she'd filmed herself doing the job, finding some balance inside herself, and some peace.

Once she and Nola had decided on this path, it had felt right. Like exactly what she needed. She knew she'd sort of lied to Conrad about why she was here. No use mentioning the old boyfriend who was getting married in her hometown. She also knew saying she didn't want to be like her mom had a lot to do with the fact that she'd secretly hoped she *was* like her mom and had found the love of her life.

When Wayne had rejected her, moved on so quickly and gotten engaged…well, Lansdowne hadn't felt like home anymore. Her producers had suggested they remodel another town and she'd jumped at the chance to be somewhere new.

Gilbert Corners.

She genuinely liked the people here, even the town council when they'd been difficult about her ideas for the park cleanup and the spring fling. She knew a big part of that was the image she had of small towns in her head. It didn't help that she had grown up watching *Gilmore Girls* and then fallen further for small towns viewing *Schitt's Creek*. Those shows had given her a glimpse of something she'd never realized she wanted.

She glanced at her phone. She'd sneakily taken a screen shot of the video call last night, so she opened it after making sure no one could see her and clicked on the saved photo of Conrad.

In the dim light of his bedroom, one side of his features were in shadow. She traced her finger over the jagged scar that disappeared into his beard and zoomed in to look more closely at his eyes, trying to read his emotions. It was hard to say for certain, but she saw passion and need in them. She sighed.

"What are you doing?"

She jumped and screamed. "Nola, you scared me."

"Yeah, I can see that. You seemed lost in thought," she said, craning her neck to see the screen.

Indy quickly hit the button to close the phone and stuffed it into her pocket. "What's up?"

"Thought I'd see if you wanted to take a lunch break," she said. "I stopped by the deli on my way here—the owners want to talk to you about filming its renovations. They have some good ideas. I took a look around the place and have some photos if you want to look at them."

"Great. I have my eye on the old general store/ five-and-ten space. But that is going to be a big job. So the deli might be a nice place to film and get the town involved even more."

She led the way back to the office. After Nola had closed the door and they were both seated, Indy at her desk and Nola in the guest chair, they conference called her producer to discuss options. The production team wanted to meet the next weekend, but Indy had promised it to Conrad, and for the first time since she started the show she decided to keep that day for herself. Everyone was surprised she wasn't available but just agreed on a later date for the in-person talks.

"What are you doing this weekend? I've literally never heard you say no," Nola said.

"I know. But Conrad is taking me to his place in New York and he's going to fix me dinner," she said as Nola handed her a pastrami on rye sandwich.

"That's…wait, when did he do that?"

"Last night. He called me close to midnight," she said.

"Uh, that's interesting. So this thing between you two is more than just a kiss?" she asked.

Indy wrapped one arm around her own waist trying to hold in her excitement. It wasn't as simple as she wished it were. "Honestly, I don't know, and I'm not sure what to expect. Or if I'll even be chill enough to enjoy myself with him. But I want to go."

"I don't blame you. I mean, he *is* hot. All the Gilberts are so beautiful. Why are the rich also pretty? Seems like an unfair distribution of resources to me."

Indy laughed. "He is hot. I haven't been this turned on by a guy in real life since… Wayne. Which worries me—I don't want to make him into someone he's not just to make myself feel better."

Nola put her sandwich down and came over to hug Indy. "It's okay to give it a few minutes thought, but don't let it overwhelm you. You said you've found yourself again. And I can see that. This move has changed you. It's like…well, like you're the woman I met in the freshman dorm who was ready to set the world on fire."

She hugged her friend back. "I feel like I'm different too. I thought I was back to myself once I got the show and everything, but looking back, I think I was still swimming through life, not really living. Isn't it funny how long everything takes?"

"I mean I thought at twenty-one that's me, done, and here I am at thirty, still single, still working in a coffee shop—"

"You own the coffee shop for one thing, and you're an immensely popular part of our TV show and you have your woodworking," Indy interrupted her friend.

"Career-wise I'm right where I want to be. Romantically… I could get with a couple of guys in town if I wanted to. But just hooking up isn't really doing it for me."

"I've seen that in you lately. But I do think you

are living your best life and doing what you love," Indy said.

"Thanks. I think I am too, but we were talking about you," Nola reminded her.

"I'm trying. Every day I feel a little bit closer to figuring out what my best life looks like. I do love the TV show which I thought was a stopgap, but now it feels like what I was meant to do."

"I think it's just being comfortable in your skin," Nola said.

They finished eating their lunch, talking about the latest period drama television series that they'd both binged. After Nola left, Indy couldn't help thinking of what she'd said. Was simply being comfortable in her skin all that she needed?

Dash had stayed most of the afternoon, then left, and Conrad had come to the test kitchen. It was situated in an old warehouse that he'd converted a few blocks from his Michelin starred restaurant La Bête de la Fable. He had done most of his kitchen training in France and all of his recipes were twists on classic French dishes.

Recently though, he'd been leaning more into fusion, which he knew could go either way with the Michelin judges, and the head chef, Lucien, and his partner, Sig, both were wary of doing anything risky. Risk was like second nature to him at this point, but he knew that his livelihood wasn't tied to the success or failure of the restaurant the way his staff's and partner's lives were.

Yet he couldn't help pushing himself. And he was back again trying to find a dish that would help him make sense of Indy. Last night he'd had a different glimpse of her, with her hair hanging down and curling around her face. The dark curls against her lighter skin had made him think of sorrel and mushrooms in a thick cream sauce. There was something so homey and satisfying about that combination.

So he'd start with that as a base. She'd stirred fire and heat in him, so he gravitated toward garlic and maybe some chilies or ginger. He pulled the spices walking through his kitchen pantry and trying to think what else. She was delicate, and a cream sauce required something else delicate…not chicken, which was too commonplace for Indy. Something more exciting and intoxicating. His mind kept running through ingredients; before he could make his choice the door to the test kitchen opened and Ophelia walked in.

"I was surprised to see your bike out front today," she said. "But glad. We need to talk about the challenge."

She looked understated and sophisticated as always. She wore a pencil skirt and T-shirt that had sequins where her breasts were. He never knew what he was going to get with Ophelia. She loved to experiment with fashion, he had realized a long time ago that her clothes were an indicator of her mood. He just never had been sure what that mood was. .

"What about it?"

"I have been editing the footage. Do you want me to take out the part about you going to the spring renewal? I also found another challenger for you. You free this weekend?" she asked. "The chef who issued the challenge is one the network is thinking of offering a show to, so it would be a nice test run."

Well fuck.

He was tempted to say yes. Maybe it was fate as Indy believed, stepping in to save her from him. But he wanted her, and fate was going to have work harder than this.

"Sorry, but I can't. Leave the spring renewal thing in. I think one of the kids in town put a video of it up on his socials—Dash is monitoring it if you want to add the footage to the end of the show. I'll film with your other guy as well, but just not this weekend."

"You never have weekend plans."

Ophelia and he had spent more than one late night drinking and sharing stories of their pasts. Both of them came from a different world than cooking and restaurants and were glad to have left it behind.

He ignored that.

"I'll let the network know that you'll do a remote pickup for the promos and cook with their guy in a ten-minute spot. That area is famous for fried bologna rolls, so try to plan on doing a take on that."

"Are you serious?"

"Am I ever not?" She paused. "What are you working on, anyway?"

"Not sure yet. Something that's been in my mind and elusive on my tongue. I know the taste I want to achieve, but haven't figured out what's needed yet," he said.

"Good luck with that. I'll send out the shooting schedule tonight so you can prepare. Let me know if you need anything," she said before waving goodbye and leaving.

Yesterday, talking to Indy had made him realize that the hatred he'd been carrying around toward his grandfather had started to wane. Maybe it stemmed from the fact that he'd found a life he liked. Cooking suited him in way that nothing else ever had. And the commercial kitchens he'd worked in had given him a place to rage around as much as he wanted to. They were intense and tempers flared, and words flew but were easily forgiven. He'd found a way to live with his beast in the kitchen.

Now he just had to figure out how to do that outside it. This weekend with Indy…maybe he was taking a step toward that. Inviting her to come and see his neighborhood. Having guests in the house he'd grown up in was something of a gamble. Only Dash visited him there. He didn't entertain, and he knew that he was more himself there than anywhere else. It would be harder to contain his base instincts.

But he would have to.

He didn't want to take a chance on scaring her

off, not now when he had her so close. He'd spent the last ten years trying to move on from that horrible night and slowly, small parts of him had, but this was something different.

This was him thinking about a woman, and not just for sex. This was him thinking about a relationship, and though he was a man who didn't allow himself to be afraid of anything, he also wouldn't lie to himself. Something about Indy scared him. He'd used his beastly persona to prevent himself from forming close attachments but none of those things had kept him from starting to care for her.

That felt more dangerous than anything he'd experienced before.

Nine

Indy was surprised when the limo pulled up in front of her house at eight on Saturday morning. Conrad had texted her to ask if she could be ready early, so maybe she shouldn't have been. The driver came to the door and she looked down at her wedge-heeled sandals and the large leather carryall where she'd packed for the weekend on her shoulder and wondered if she was underdressed.

"Ms. Belmont, are you ready?"

"Yes, sir," she said, closing and locking her door behind her.

The chauffeur opened the rear door and she was surprised to find the backseat empty. She'd expected Conrad. But she sat down and scooted into the air-conditioned car. The screen was down between her and the driver and she seemed to remember that proper etiquette dictated the passenger decide if they wanted privacy or not.

She waited until he was seated before leaning forward.

"Is Mr. Gilbert joining us?"

"He asked me to escort you to Gilbert Manor where he's waiting for you."

She leaned back. Obviously, something had changed since last they'd spoken. He had offered to show her around his neighborhood in the city. She sat back as the car drove through the town of Gilbert Corners and then turned left out of town and drove up the winding hills that led to Gilbert Manor.

The main roads had been maintained, but when they turned off them, they became less neat. They drove through Doric columns that supported a marble arch with the name Gilbert on it. The landscaping on both sides of the drive had been maintained, but she could hear the gravel under the tires until they rounded a corner, and the tree-lined drive gave way to a circular solid brick drive that led up to a large portico entrance. There was another man standing at the front door in a dark suit.

Again, not Conrad.

The house was intimidating her a little this time. It wasn't like when she'd been here for the cook-off. She was clearly a guest of "Mr. Gilbert." Not Conrad. Not her dear beast.

He opened the door as the car pulled to a stop and

offered her his hand, which she took as she climbed out of the back of the limo.

"Welcome to Gilbert Manor, Ms. Belmont. I am Worthington, head of household. Mr. Gilbert asked that I show you inside to your room."

"I'm not sure I'm staying overnight," she said, though she'd packed for it.

"It's just for the day, so you can freshen up."

She just nodded. The drive wasn't that far, but when she entered the house, she caught her breath and stopped worrying about Conrad and what was going on. The foyer looked like marble to her untrained eye, and the arches she'd seen back at the entrance were mirrored here.

In fact, the entry hall was wide, bigger than her living room and elegantly appointed. There was a grand staircase in the center with hallways that led off in both directions. Worthington told her the history of the house as he led the way up the stairs, but she wasn't paying attention. Instead, her eyes were drawn to the portraiture on the walls. There was a striking resemblance between Gilbert and his ancestors.

Worthington stopped down the left hall in front of a door. "Here is your room. Mr. Gilbert wanted to give you some space. I'll wait outside until you are ready and then escort you to join him in the library."

She went into the bedroom, pulled out her phone and called Conrad.

"Yes."

"What's going on? I thought you hated Gilbert Manor and everything about where you grew up."

"I don't hate it all. This place is probably more directly responsible for who I am than the house I lived in with my parents. Is it too formal? I mean, I would get it if you didn't like it."

She looked around the elegant room with the four-poster bed and Chippendale furniture. She noticed a dress on the bed that looked light as air, all tulle and satin, and she went closer to examine it.

"I don't know. And what's the dress for?" She ran her hand over it. It wasn't the kind of thing she'd ever worn. She never got to walk the red carpet, and she'd never been invited to a ball. This was…too much.

"It's too much for a day date."

"Dinner. We always dress for meals at the manor. Plus, maybe this is what's needed for us to break the curse."

"You said you didn't believe in it," she pointed out.

"I don't, but let's say there is a curse—it probably started the night of the ball and the car crash," he said. "I guess I'll have to leave the ballroom with a gorgeous woman to break it."

Then just left it there. "How about we have this tour and then we see how the day goes?" she said.

"We'll start off slow then. There are some riding clothes in the armoire. Do you ride?"

"Not since Girl Scout camp, and then it was a tethered ride."

"Do you trust me to keep you safe?" he asked.

She did. She wouldn't be here if she didn't. "I do. But your head of household mentioned a library. Can I see that before we go riding?"

"Yes. If you want, we can skip riding and have a picnic on the terrace next to the library," he said.

"I want!"

"Then come as you are," he said.

She started for the door, but stopped. "What are you wearing?"

"Why?"

"I mean are you in some tux or formal wear?"

"I'll be casual when you get here," he said.

She put her bag on the bed, freshened up her hair and makeup and went out into the hallway about ten minutes later to find Conrad waiting for her.

She looked at his face, with the scar on one side, his hair wild around his head…but his smile was tentative. He wasn't as sure of himself as she'd seen him in the past. Why had he brought her here? What was he trying to show her—more of himself, or was it something he was trying to prove to himself?

She had a feeling that some of his discomfort was rooted in the fact that he wasn't the same man he had been the last time he was here. Like he had said, the night of the ball that started the curse. She wondered if, like herself, Conrad had two lives he was trying to stitch together to make one whole.

For her, it came back to that horrible sexual attack from her date. The two women she was—one before and one after—were slowly becoming one, stronger woman. Conrad from all accounts had been arrogant and very lord-of-the-manor before the accident and then he became the person she saw today. Was he trying to bridge those two pieces?

If so, she wanted to help him find a way. Not that she was an expert.

"I like the place. You make more sense here," she said.

Conrad had given a lot of thought to what Dash had said. He couldn't treat Indy the way he had everyone else in his adult life. Well he *could*, but late last night it had occurred to him that if he did, he'd regret it. There was something about her, and he'd never been a man to walk away from a new experience.

So he'd gone all in. Indy meant spending more time in Gilbert Corners and he needed to wrestle with the demons from his past. While he did think the town belief in a curse was total BS, there was a glimmer of something to it.

That night had really changed his life forever.

He needed to find a way to make peace with it, something that he wasn't sure he could accomplish. Being back in the house had reminded him of memories he'd shoved deep down and covered up. Good memories of running down the halls with Dash and Rory. Planning cookie and pie heists, and helping Worthington by sliding down the banisters so he wouldn't have to polish them.

He smiled as Indy stood next to him. He'd thrown her off by changing their plans at the last minute, which was something he liked to do when he was nervous. He wanted to see if it rattled her. No surprise, the change of venue hadn't.

He liked the grin in her eyes as she called this palatial manor house a "nice place."

"Want the grand tour?" he asked.

"Worthington gave me some of it, but I was distracted," she admitted.

"There's no rush. You did promise me the entire weekend," he said.

"True. Then can we start with the portraits in the entry foyer?" she asked. "Who are all those people? You look like some of them."

She was interested in his past, and he realized he was going to have to crack open and let her see parts of himself. The portraits in the hall were nice, but the gallery above the ballroom would be more impressive.

"Let me show you where we keep the important people," he said, putting his hand on her back and leading her down the hall to the gallery. It was a large balcony with a gold-plated guardrail that overlooked the rotunda that was the ballroom.

The ceiling was a fresco that had been painted in the 1920s by a contemporary painter who had blended the abstract with modern cubism.

"Wow, that's impressive. Is the ceiling supposed to be…actually, I can't make it out? I'm not really good at guessing abstract designs."

He laughed. "Me either. Dash and I decided that the darkish part on this side was where the evil dragons or Pokémon lived when we were kids, and we would battle them around the walkway to the other side where it's lighter. They'd be banished, and we'd win."

"I like it. Is it meant to be a sky?"

"Yes. It's the artist's view of Gilbert Corners' sky in all the seasons apparently. Rory used to know a bunch of facts about it," he said.

"Do you miss her?" she asked.

He didn't like talking about her. But that was why he'd brought Indy here. He needed to see if he could open up. He wanted to let her in. "Yes."

"Do you want to talk about her?"

"No."

She slipped her hand into his and squeezed. A heat spread up his arm then through him and though he'd vowed to take things slow today, he knew he wanted her. Had wanted to pull her into his arms since the moment she'd stepped out of her room.

"That's okay. So who are the people in the portraits behind us?" she asked, dropping his hand and turning to the framed picture.

He stood behind her and put his arm on her shoulder, pulling her back into his body. "This is the first Gilbert family who settled here. They came over from England to help settle this colony."

He kept his arm around her shoulders as he led her circling the rotunda showing her his ancestors through the years, stopping in front of the portrait with him and his parents. He hadn't looked at it in years. In fact, when he and Dash had played up here, they always ignored these most recent pictures.

She slipped her arm around his waist. "Are those your parents?"

"Hmm."

She turned so that her body was pressed to his side as she hugged him. "You must miss them. You look just like your dad, but you have your mother's eyes."

He hugged her back, both comforted and turned on by her touch. He held her and finally lifted his eyes to the painting. He felt his eyes sting as he looked at his mom and dad for the first time in decades. They looked so young. As a child they'd seemed old, but Conrad was almost the age his father had been when he'd died.

God, he missed them.

Indy hugged him tight and then went up on her tiptoes to kiss his cheek. He turned his head and found her mouth with his. Channeling his grief into the one emotion that he felt at home expressing. He didn't move to surround her, even dropped his arm from her shoulder but she stayed where she was.

He felt her hand on his waist tighten as her tongue brushed over his, and he opened himself to the kiss and the blooming sensuality he felt in her. He kept tight control on himself and turned slightly so her chest brushed against his torso.

She hesitated for a second, then pulled him closer against her as her hands moved down his back to cup his butt and draw him more fully against her.

The blood rushed from his brain, and he stopped thinking and started to give in to the passion, which was never far away when Indy was around. He lifted her slightly off her feet with one arm around her hips and deepened the kiss even more.

Letting loose the tight control he'd been holding on to since the moment he'd seen her today. Desire and lust had been hard to tamp down and he'd surprised himself by how much talking to Indy had just made him want her more.

He would do everything in his power to make her stay with him and to have her in his bed tonight.

She hadn't meant to kiss him, but the pain had been almost palpable when he'd looked at the portrait of him and his parents. And Indy's heart had broken for that little boy. Conrad smiled out of the portrait with innocence and pure happiness. Two things that he no longer had.

She cautioned herself to be careful with him. There was so much hidden inside him that he had just let scab over and moved on. She saw it in him because she felt it inside herself every day. They were both broken—or maybe bent, not broken, but in different ways. She didn't know that their bent pieces could fit together. She was trying to be entirely realistic. Which wasn't how she normally acted. Of course, as he deepened the kiss, lifting her off her feet so that she was leaning fully into his body with his erection growing against her, she realized there was a way that they would fit together very nicely.

But she wasn't sure she was ready to get physical with him. She wanted him, but there was still so much about him she was unsure of. It was only Conrad's sadness that he seemed to allow himself to feel. She suspected he felt something for her but could he express that? As if he somehow was trying to show her what he couldn't say directly

That was part of it. He was trying to make her feel more comfortable with him. His sadness sort of teased hers out, made the memories start to creep in. Made her remember the reasons why she was hesitating with this man that was so tempting, so intriguing. Despite her doubts it was sort of working and she wanted to just open herself and be vulnerable to him.

No matter that at times that thought scared her.

But she slammed it, pushing the past where it belonged. Far away from this otherworldly balcony surrounded by Conrad's past on one side and his rock-solid, hot body on the other. He tasted so good, like something exotic and addicting. She admitted she wanted more. Of his kisses, of his body, of everything he'd offer her.

She had the feeling deep in her gut that these moments with Conrad were fleeting. That any real chance of him staying with her wasn't realistic. But at the same time, he was offering her something no other man could. A chance to reclaim a part of her femininity that she'd been afraid of for much too long.

He lifted his head, staring down into her eyes, and she wanted to be cool. Wanted to make it seem as if this was just a hot kiss and there weren't a million other emotions rolling through her, but she knew she didn't pull it off when he rubbed his thumb over her bottom lip and gave her a knowing smile.

"I think we've seen enough of my family," he said. "So next stop is up to you. Library or the gardens?" he asked.

She was disappointed at how relieved she was that he'd made this moment normal. But at the same time, this was one of the things that made it hard for her not to fall for Conrad. Her mind was blaring the word *temporary*, but her heart and soul felt this connection that seemed eternal.

"Library first," she said. "I'm going to be fully disappointed if it isn't at least floor-to-ceiling and doesn't have a ladder."

"Oh, you'll have to wait and see," he said, leading her away from the rotunda. Before they stepped off the walkway, she stopped him.

"Is this where the ball was?"

She felt almost as if a curtain had come down between them. He gave her a tight-lipped nod.

"It's so pretty. I bet it looked nice that night," she said carefully. She was backpedaling, trying not to push too hard, but that kiss had blown past the barriers that she'd thought she'd put in place. And even if he was temporary…would it really hurt to ask the hard questions?

"It was. You can see it from here if you look closely—there are a bunch of fiber-optic lights in the ceiling that make it look like twinkling stars," he said.

"Sounds magical," she observed. If she pushed for anything else, he'd shut her out completely. "Like the perfect night for a curse to be born."

"Probably," he said. "I guess that makes my grandfather some sort of evil wizard."

"Maybe, or maybe a jealous witch put a spell on the castle and everyone in it."

"It's a manor house," he pointed out.

"You just said it was magical."

"Did I say that? Seems more like you were the one going for the magic angle."

"Well this is way more castle-like than any house I've lived in," she said.

"I'll allow it."

She lightly punched his shoulder, delighted at the resistance of his solid muscles. She pulled her hand back. "Do you work out?"

He started laughing and shook his head. "Yes. If I don't then I fall into bad habits."

"Like?"

"Indulging your questions," he said.

"I know you count on those kinds of responses to shut me up, but it won't work," she said. "Did your dad grow up here?"

"He did. Dash and Rory's father was his twin," he said.

"When did his mom die?" she asked. "I'm wondering if that's what happened to change your grandfather."

"Don't try to make him human to me."

She took a deep breath. This was pushing in a way

that she couldn't justify. She should leave it alone. But she liked Conrad, she wanted him and he was making her think of things that she hadn't dreamed of in a long time. So that meant she was going to have to take a few risks.

But for now she'd leave it.

She was also curious about his grandmother. From all accounts his father was a good, loving man. Which meant at some point, someone in this house had been loving too.

She had a lot of questions, but kept them to herself.

"So the library?"

"Down this way," he said, leading them to the stairs. He put some physical distance between the two of them and she couldn't help wondering if he regretted inviting her here.

But she didn't ask and when they got to the library, she forgot all about that. It was full of floor-to-ceiling bookcases with ladders to reach the top shelves. There were overstuffed chairs positioned in the room and a window seat that overlooked the gardens in the back of the house.

"You do not disappoint, Conrad," she said.

"Stick around. I'm just getting started."

Ten

Conrad wasn't used to second-guessing himself. It just wasn't the way he operated. He moved forward and left regret behind him. But having Indy here wasn't the smartest idea. She stirred fierce emotions like affection and caring. He struggled to deal with them, as he hadn't really allowed himself to care for anyone other than Rory and Dash for a decade. Whether she meant to or not, Indy was making him feel.

She didn't respond to his comment and he was happy enough for that. She moved into the library, which had large French doors that overlooked the patio and then the gardens below. But she didn't move toward them. Instead she went to the bookshelves.

Just given what he'd seen of her shop, he wasn't

surprised that she liked books. This wasn't his favorite room in the house and normally he avoided it but he wanted to make her smile. And he had. It was worth the too tight feeling of his skin.

She stood in front of the bookcase that housed some of the oldest and rarest collections of his family's books. There was a genealogy of the Gilberts that went all the way back to a foolscap illuminated manuscript from the late 1400s up to today, which of course was leatherbound. He skipped past his family history to the bookshelf in the corner that had been his father's favorite.

Unless he was drunk, he rarely allowed himself to think of his parents. But seeing their photo today had reminded him of this corner. He stooped down and, on the bottom shelf, pulled out a copy of *The Three Musketeers* by Alexandre Dumas. He held it loosely in one hand, reaching into the space created. He had to feel around for it, but then he caught the braided cord of the hidden book.

He pulled it out just as Indy wandered over to him. He stood up as she approached.

"What have you got there?" she asked.

"*Three Musketeers*. It was my dad's favorite."

"And that?" she asked pointing to the small, bound sheaf of papers held in his other hand.

He lifted it up to show her. "Something my dad and his brother wrote when they were younger. Dash and I found it one rainy summer day. I had forgotten about it until now."

She came closer and put her hand on his arm. The

touch went through him like fire and he started to pull away, but then stopped himself. What if Indy wasn't different from other women? What if it was just his reaction to her? What if he was somehow making her into something he needed?

And if that was the case, maybe he should stop trying to see her in a different light. He put his arm around her shoulder and pulled her into the curve of his body. She seemed startled at first and then she put her arm around his waist.

"*The Adventures of Blue and Brown*…not the best title in the world," she said.

"Yeah. Dad and Uncle Hamm were fraternal twins and had different color eyes…so that's where the title comes from," he said.

"Want to read it to me?" she suggested, taking his hand again and leading him over to the window seat.

He followed her, very aware that he wasn't feeling stable. Like he was on the cusp of something. It didn't feel like anger, but anger was his old home and the most comfortable of his emotions. This was different, and he wasn't going to deny that it scared him. She sat down on one side and drew her legs up to her chest before resting her chin on them, watching him.

His chest felt too tight and his body was on fire for her. The touches and this closeness were making it almost impossible to think of anything other than pulling her into his arms. No one would disturb them and making love on the large window seat appealed to him.

"Scoot up. I'll sit behind you," he said.

She nodded and moved forward and after a moment he was seated behind her. His legs cradling either side of her body, her back pressed against his chest, her buttocks right against his cock. He put his arms around her and opened the homemade book.

"'*The Adventures of Blue and Brown* started on a cold, wet Wednesday when the cook made blueberry pie.'"

He read the story to her of two boys scheming to steal a pie from the kitchen and their misfortune as they got closer and closer and were always foiled by someone or something. They couldn't take a direct route to the kitchens since it went past their father's study and he was working. It ended with them being called down to dinner and their mother giving them both a slice of pie.

He'd never known his grandmother. She'd died when his dad was in high school. But reading this… if he had to guess where his father's kindness had come from, it was definitely her.

"That was fun," she said. "You have a great reading voice. I think you should consider doing some sort of audio thing."

"Yeah?"

"Hmm mmm," she said, turning around so that she knelt between his legs. "Why did you did you bring me here?"

He glanced down at the curve of her neckline where the slight swell of her breasts was visible and then back up to her face. Why? He wasn't entirely sure. But he knew he had to say something.

"I don't know. I want you," he said with blunt honesty. "And you are tied to this town and not a casual person. And I hate this place…so I figured I should try to see if I could like it here."

"Is it working?" she asked.

He wasn't entirely sure of that. "I still want you."

"I want you too," she said. "I've only had sex with one person…before that date that went wrong."

He nodded; that made sense to him.

"Do you want to talk about it?"

"Not really. I wasn't feeling it and said no and he…didn't stop."

Despite what he'd been trying to convince himself of earlier, she wasn't a like any other woman. He knew that. She was passionate and put herself into all things that mattered to her. And that made him want her even more.

The fact that she wasn't casual might be why he wanted her so badly. Why he felt something more for her other than lust, and why he'd brought her here. He might have told himself and acted to the world like he wanted no part of Gilbert Manor or even Gilbert Corners, but the truth was more nuanced than that.

He hadn't been able to admit it until Indy. She was making him see himself and this place in a different way. He wasn't entirely sure he liked it but he also knew he couldn't walk away from her.

"I've had lots of sex and different partners but none of them have been you," he admitted.

She looked into Conrad's big blue eyes and fancied that she could see into his soul. But the truth was more complex than that. He was a man who didn't share himself easily or at all. Since she'd arrived here—actually, since his car had shown up at her house, the day hadn't gone the way she'd expected. She could tell that Conrad wasn't as in control as he usually was.

It was nice to see his guard drop. She hadn't been lying about his gorgeous reading voice; there was a sensitivity to him that he kept carefully hidden. She had a glimpse of it when he'd cooked for her. He was the kind of man who always had his guard up. And hearing how his father and uncle had trodden carefully around their grandfather gave her more of an idea of why he was that way.

He'd been surrounding her while he read, and she had found that his voice was now as much as part of her as her heartbeat or breathing. She wanted him.

"Is there anything in your sexual health history I should know?"

He shook his head, smiling at her. "No. Nothing at all."

"Sorry, I mean it would be irresponsible not to ask. I know it's not sexy," she said.

"It's not scxy, but your straightforwardness is. And before you ask, I have condoms and I will wear one," he said.

She felt herself blushing but nodded her thanks. She had been planning to ask. They were in a new relationship and still figuring things out. It might not go further than this one day in Gilbert Manor. Neither of them needed the complication of an unexpected pregnancy.

"Great."

"Come on. I want to cook for you in a kitchen that's actually stocked. What's your favorite meal?" he asked, lifting her up and swinging his legs to the floor. He set her on her feet before standing and leading her out of the library.

"Can we come back here later? I didn't get to look at all the books," she said.

"Of course. Favorite meal?"

The hallway they walked through wasn't as formal as the one they'd entered through. She tried to think of her favorite meal, but he was a chef with a Michelin star and a television show, so she wanted to make it sound like a real meal instead of Kraft Mac & Cheese with cut up hot dogs. She tried to remember the best meal she'd had, and it was either her dad's barbecue or her mom's hush puppies.

"It's nothing sophisticated," she admitted.

"It's okay. I like all kinds of food."

She was sure that meant exotic stuff that she'd probably have to force herself to eat. She just wasn't a foodie. "What's *your* favorite meal?"

"Why are you hesitating?" he asked.

She stopped walking and put one arm around her waist. "I don't want to say something else that will just make you realize how much I don't fit in with your life."

He put one hand on the wall behind her head and the other on her shoulder as he leaned in. "I'm the one who doesn't fit. That's why I'm here."

She reached up to touch his face because she'd

been longing to do that since he'd stopped reading. "Maybe we fit because we're so different?"

"Maybe. Food is how I…well, how I communicate best. Even Dash has said it and honestly, he's the one person I'm closest to."

"My favorite meals are my dad's barbecue, my mom's hush puppies and boxed macaroni and cheese," she said. "I'm also a fan of fast-food chicken sandwiches. Those foods all connect to my happiest memories. Sometimes it was the aftermath of disappointment but those meals…"

"I get it. Food is love," he said as he started to walk again and she followed him.

"Did I shock you with my basic food loves?"

"No. I like barbecue too and hush puppies. The only food I don't really eat is fast food," he said.

She had a friend in New York who had never had fast food, so that didn't surprise her. She couldn't imagine him eating in that kind of place. "So what are you going to make?"

"I'm not sure yet," he said. "But I've got a few ideas."

"Like what?"

"Something simple."

"Simple?"

"Don't say it like that's an insult. The best meals are simple. Made with fresh ingredients."

"Like those cheese sandwiches you made for us," she said. "I had no idea those ingredients from my fridge could taste that good."

"Yeah, well, this will be better than that," he added.

“I don’t see how,” she said as he led her into the kitchen and motioned for her to have a seat at the long butcher-block island. There was a stool set up and she realized that he’d planned this.

This was truly Conrad’s world and she believed she’d learn a lot about him in here. She told herself that was what she wanted, but she already liked him more than was healthy and that possibly this wasn’t her smartest idea.

“I’m thinking a creamy pasta, maybe with a smokey element.”

“Sounds great. Where do you keep the pasta? I’ll make that.”

“I don’t have dried pasta,” he said. “I’m going to make it fresh. Want to learn?”

She did. “I’m not a very good cook.”

“You say that but the biscuits you made at the cook-off were delicious. I think you’re better at it than you let on.”

“Thanks. I deliberately didn’t cook at my best during our challenge and let you win.”

He gave a loud laugh and shook his head as she started to pull ingredients together. She knew that she was never going to be at his level but there was something about watching him that made her realize how much passion and joy he brought in the kitchen. Cooking seemed to bring down all of his barriers. It was all she could do to stay where she was and not go and wrap herself around him. She wanted this afternoon to be one of her best memories and hoped that it would be.

Hoped that she could find a way to keep her cool and make the most of her time with him. He had awakened her desire and it was impossible to watch Conrad in the kitchen and not get turned on.

He was seducing her without realizing it. Watching his hands move as he took a bunch of herbs made her want to feel his hands on her skin. This was a slow, sensual seduction of her and her senses.

Food had been the only thing that he could use to distract himself from Indy.

He didn't cook with anyone. But because there were words he knew he couldn't say and emotions he was struggling to show her, cooking for her was the safest way for him to be his authentic self. He wanted her to see him here where he felt the most comfortable in his skin. He was pretty much a nightmare to work for in the kitchen because he had exacting standards, but he wanted to show her how to cook. Wanted to extend that feeling he'd had in the library when he'd held her in his arms and thought about her naked body under his.

He showed her how to measure the flour and make a well for it on the bench and then did the same for his own pasta. They wouldn't be able to eat this much pasta on their own, but he'd give the rest to Jenkins the groundskeeper.

"Next, crack an egg in the middle of the well."

He did it with one hand and turned toward her as he heard her tapping the egg on the side of the counter three times. Then she broke it and poured it into the center. He took the shells from her and tossed them in the sink without looking back.

"Now it's time to get messy. Use your fingers to incorporate the egg and flour."

She started to do it; as the flour and egg got caked on her fingers, he saw her struggle. He moved to stand behind her, before putting his arms around her. He took her hand in his and showed her the right motion. She smelled like summer flowers, distracting him. Her body fit perfectly in the cradle of his. He felt himself hardening. He let his erection brush against her, her hips rubbed against him. His reaction was to get even harder.

He knew she'd been scared by a man, knew that was part of it, but also, he was beginning to think maybe he was punishing himself by putting her off limits. He leaned down and brushed his mouth against her neck. The scent of flowers was stronger here. She turned her hand under his, their fingers meshing together on the table as she rolled her head and looked up at him.

Their eyes met and he realized he'd held off as long as he could. He wanted her. He wanted more than cooking or trying to slowly seduce her. He wasn't a slow seduction sort of man. "Do you want this?"

She nodded.

But he needed to hear her say it. He wasn't going to guess at anything with Indy. She meant too much for him to fuck this up now.

"Yes?"

"Yes," she said.

He lifted her up on the counter and stepped between her legs, spreading them as he did so. He put his hands on the sides of her waist and pulled her forward so that her legs were on either side of his torso. They were eye level like this. She rested her forehead against his and he felt the exhalation of her breath against his mouth and then the touch of her tongue over his lips.

He hardened even more as he took the kiss he'd wanted all day. It was long and deep, intimate, and left no place for either one of them to hide. Her hands moved up his back and he felt one hand in his hair as she shifted forward, wrapping her thigh around his hips trying to get closer to him.

He put one hand behind her on the butcher-block counter and lifted himself up so that he could rub his erection against her center. He lifted his head, realizing he needed more room. He wanted her naked and spread out under him.

"Wrap your legs around me," he said. His voice sounded rough and guttural to his own ears.

She did as he asked, wrapping her arms around his shoulders as well. He turned them and carried her up the stairs to the bedroom she'd put her bag in earlier. She caressed his shoulders as he carried her, and when they were in the room, he set her on her feet and closed the door behind them. He toed off his shoes and reached for her, then pulled her back into his arms.

She went eagerly, her hands going to the buttons of his shirt and undoing them; her fingers brushed against his chest with each button she undid. He let her finish unbuttoning his shirt and then shrugged out of it. He felt her fingers moving over his body. He knew that the tattoos might visually cover it, but with her touch she'd feel the roughness of his scarred body.

He stood still. Normally when he fucked, he did it with his clothes on and standing up, keeping as much of himself hidden from his partner. Making sex into a need instead of a want. But he wanted Indy's bare body against his naked skin. He didn't want to keep anything hidden. .

He wanted to explore all of her and he hadn't thought about how intimate it would be for her to explore him.

Her fingers followed the patterns on his skin, and then she leaned forward and he felt her mouth on his neck. She dropped small kisses all down the column of his neck to his chest. Moving across the front and then under his arm around to his back. Where the worst of the damage was. The nerves of his lower back were shot, and he was numb there, but he almost felt her touch.

She came back around and looked up at him. What he saw in her eyes, he didn't want to hear spoken out loud. So, he lifted her in his arms again, bringing his mouth down hard on hers. Kissing her so deeply that she couldn't think, just feel. Feel him against her. He put her down on the side of the four-poster bed.

He started to come down on top of her, but she scooted back, and he realized she wasn't ready for that. So he undid his pants and then sat down on the bed, with his back resting on the backboard.

"Come sit on my lap," he said.

She nodded and moved forward straddling him. "I'm sorr—

"Don't. There's no need for that between the two of us," he said to her.

Words weren't going to fix either one of them. But maybe sex could. Maybe sex would give them both what they needed. And maybe he would be free of this obsession with her.

Eleven

Nerves and desire warred within her. It was impossible to see Conrad's tattoo-covered body and think of anything other than being in his arms and feeling him inside of her. The top half of his body was heavily muscled; his strength enticed her like nothing else had. The intricate pattern of thorny branches encased him the way she wanted to with her body. She leaned forward, tracing her fingers over the pattern, acutely aware of his thick erection between her legs.

She took her clothes off as she watched him. There were so many times when she had been struck by the similarities between them, but now she celebrated the differences in them. His height and mass against her smaller frame were something she had initially worried about, but he kept himself tightly leashed. There was nothing out of control about him. Which made her feel safe in a way she hadn't realized she needed.

There was something so reassuring about Conrad and his control. He wanted her, but if she changed her mind, she knew that Conrad wouldn't force himself on her. That was freeing in a way that nothing else could be.

She lowered her head and traced the path her fingers had taken with her tongue. He tasted a bit salty and his skin was warm. She heard the ragged intake of his breath as she scooted back on his thighs and moved lower across his torso. His stomach was ridged with muscles and she had to admit, she liked it. Personally she'd never wanted to be muscly or work out, but she was glad he did.

She felt his hand in her hair, massaging her scalp, and then his other arm moved languidly around her, tracing a seemingly random pattern on her back and shoulder and then his touch moved to her collarbone. She held her own breath as his neared her breast. His thumb stroked over her nipple and she felt it harden, and her breasts became heavier and fuller with need. She turned her head. Noticed that thick cock between his legs and shifted around so she could touch it with her tongue as she closed her hand around his shaft.

He arched his hips slightly and she took just the tip of him into her mouth. Then she sucked him in deeper as she stroked him. Her other hand moved to his balls, squeezing them lightly as his thumb continued to rub back and forth across her nipple. She felt his big hand on her butt. First cupping one cheek, and then his fingers lightly tracing between her cheeks. She clenched her pussy as she dampened. His fingers moved lower but still so slowly.

She continued to suck him deeper into her mouth but her attention was torn between his big cock and his fingers on her most intimate flesh. He drew his finger light around the opening of her body and she spread her legs a bit wider but he just still moved around the opening. She squeezed his sac and then took him deeper into her throat, enjoying the feeling of him in her mouth and the way he reacted. His thumb on her nipple stopped moving and he arched underneath her again.

She smiled to herself, enjoying the feeling of having this big man under her control. She moved closer to the side of his body as she could take more of him in her mouth and continue to drive him crazy with lust.

He shifted on the bed and she felt him lift one of her legs to slide between them. His mouth was on her feminine center, parting the folds of her body and finding her clit with his tongue. He flicked it over her; her own mouth went slack on his erection as sensual flames licked through her. She arched her own hips trying to get more of his mouth.

But he just kept licking her, as if he had all the time in the world. She wanted more. But Conrad wasn't going to be rushed. She sucked harder on his cock and his hips started moving under her, just two thrusts before he pulled himself back and free of her mouth. He tumbled her onto her back, his hands coming to her hips to hold her on the bed as his mouth stayed busy between her legs.

"Conrad..."

"Shh...let me give this to you," he said against her skin. She shivered at the heat of his breath against her clit, and the sound of his words resonated within her body, sending a deep shaft of desire through her.

She arched her back, putting her hands in his thick hair and holding his head to her as she lifted herself into the lashings of his tongue. He continued to trace her pussy with his other finger. She couldn't take much more teasing when he pushed his finger up into her body.

She cried out his name as her walls tightened around it, twisting her fingers in his hair and holding him to her body as her orgasm washed over her. His mouth stayed busy between her legs until her thighs fell wide open. She tried to pull him up her body, but he just stayed where he was.

His fingers still inside of her, he turned his head looking up. As their eyes met, she knew that something was happening between them that she wasn't ready for. Not sex. Not the intimacy that came with sharing her body with him, but something else. Something deeper that she felt all the way to her soul.

Something that, if she were honest, she couldn't define. But as she reached for his shoulders and tried to draw him up, she realized that there was a part of her that never wanted to let him go.

Even if he couldn't be hers.

Despite the fact that he was fun and this felt like

the start of something new, they were both too damaged for a relationship between them to work. He needed someone who could help reach the innocence he'd lost and she needed…well, when as he kissed her belly button and his hands closed over her breasts, his palms rubbing her nipples and making that slow burn start again low in her body, she wasn't sure *what* she needed. Part of her thought it was him. But the smarter part knew it couldn't be.

Conrad had almost come in her mouth, which hadn't been at all what he'd planned, so he'd pulled himself back from the edge. She'd tasted so good and when she'd orgasmed under his lips, that had again torn at his self-restraint but he had a deep well he drew from to keep himself under tight control. Normally sex wasn't a place where he had to fight with himself, but Indy was different.

She tasted so good. Like a dish that had all the best ingredients and flavors, including that elusive taste of umami. That fifth was heady and addictive. He was starting to crave her and admitted only to himself that he might not ever get enough of her. A smart man would only take this woman to bed once or else risk a life-long obsession to her. So he wanted to make this last.

He needed to make this last.

Wanted to explore every inch of her body and create a memory that would last the rest of his life. Because if this afternoon with Indy had shown him anything, it was that he could find a place for himself back here in GC. The only problem was him. Holding on to past hurts and grudges. He knew he should be the bigger man, but the truth was he still wasn't sure if he could be.

He knew a gentleman would start at her mouth and work down but he hadn't. And he wasn't going to deny himself any part of her body. Right now she was spread out on the bed and he was still between her legs, his hands on her small but ample breasts. He was going slowly, didn't want her to feel trapped by him. He knew he was a big man, so he wanted her to always know that she was the one truly in control.

Her hands were on his torso again, her fingers moving lower. He shifted up next to her on the bed so that he was along her side. He put one arm under her head, lifting her shoulders as he leaned down and took a dark pinkish nipple into his mouth. His other hand traced a pattern on her stomach, rubbing over her belly button as he flicked his tongue against her.

He felt her hand around his erection and knew that he wasn't going to last much longer if she kept that up. He had learned to control his responses to pain, but pleasure…this kind of pleasure was rare. When he had sex, he was legendary for his stamina…which he now realized may have been a complete lie. Her hands on his body were the best kind of aphrodisiac. And he didn't want to resist.

Why was he dragging this out? Why was he denying himself what she was so eager to give him? But the why was right there in the back of his mind.

They were dangerous for each other. It felt like they could be each other's salvation or destruction.

She pushed against him and though her touch couldn't budge him, he let her urge him over onto his back and she straddled him, her hands on his shoulders. He fondled her breasts as she did so. Their eyes met and something unspoken passed between them. For himself it was all deep affection and caring. The two things he'd thought he'd burned out of his body with partying and fighting years ago.

But Indy was showing him that he hadn't. She licked her lips and gave him a tentative smile as she positioned herself over his cock. He sat up, forcing her to wrap her legs around his hips, and the tip of his erection slipped into her pussy.

She gasped as he did. Their eyes met again and this time he forced his mind to stop and just enjoy this moment with her. He shifted his hips and pushed himself deeper into her. She was so tight and felt so damned good that his instinct was to roll over and drive himself into her again and again until they were both screaming each other's names as they came. But he took a deep breath and held himself still as she adjusted to his girth.

She kissed the spot where his shoulder and neck met. "Why are you covered in thorns?"

"To keep the pain inside," he said truthfully.

"Why—"

He brought his mouth down on hers to stop the questions, because he would tell her anything in this moment and he knew he'd regret it later. He put his hands on her butt and pulled her hips forward as he fell back on the bed. She kissed him deeply and though she was on top, he controlled the pace of their lovemaking.

He drove his hips up into her and pulled her forward with each thrust, making sure he filled every inch of her each time. She started moving faster and faster against him, and he felt that tingling feeling down the small of his back as his balls got heavier. He thrust up into her, feeling her tighten around him as she pulled her mouth from his and cried out his name in a long moan. He drove up into her again two more times and then came in a massive rush, emptying himself inside her. He continued to thrust a few more times, and then she collapsed on his chest as they both lay still, the afternoon sunshine spilling into the room over the back of her body.

His heart stopped racing and she stayed still on top of him. He stroked her back and felt something close to contentment. He didn't allow himself to dwell on the fact that he was in the one place he'd always hated, because he didn't want those feelings in here with Indy.

He wanted to forget about all of that. But then he felt her fingers on his chest, moving over the old ridges of his scars, and her question came back to him. His thorns. It was his version of a hair shirt. His way of reminding himself each time he looked in the mirror that his control was a cage around the rage and the emotions that he'd never been able to handle.

Her soft touch was showing him that his cage might not be strong enough this time.

Indy's emotions were right at the surface and her barriers were down. She felt like she'd seen something in Conrad's eyes that matched that soul-deep feeling she'd had when they'd been making love. She hated that he had wrapped his body in these thorny branches, and she wanted to understand more.

He'd said he used them to keep the pain inside. "What pain are you holding inside?"

She hadn't realized she had said it out loud until she heard her voice in the quiet of the afternoon. He stopped stroking her back, and because she was draped over him, she felt the tension in his body that hadn't been there a moment earlier. She rested her chin on his sternum and looked toward his face but all she saw was the bottom of his jaw, where there was another ragged scar.

He'd been so damaged physically. That didn't mean that his emotional scars weren't as deep. Given what he'd told her and how he acted, it didn't take Nancy Drew to figure out.

"I don't want to discuss that."

She tried not to let his words hurt her, but they did. She was feeling so open and…caring toward him, she'd expected him to feel the same. "Okay."

Now she felt silly and wanted some space. She pushed against his chest to get up but he put his hands on the small of her back and held her to him. Holding her gently but close to him and she realized that some times Conrad was going to show her how he felt with his physicality instead of his words.

"Don't leave," he said. There was an edge to his voice that she didn't recognize. Something in the tone that made her relax against him.

"Sorry I pushed."

"It's your way."

She laughed at that because it was true. And if she didn't laugh, she might cry. She hated this feeling and yet at the same time it was a relief to know that she could feel some emotions like this again. A part of her had been in hiding since that date rape incident back in college. She knew it could have been so much worse, but it had left her shattered.

She needed a man to talk to so that she didn't have to just hear all these thoughts in her own head. That voice that kept needling and picking things apart until she thought she'd scream.

She wanted to just lie in his arms and enjoy this moment, but she wasn't allowing herself to.

His hands moved again, up and down her back. She swallowed and looked up at him again, and this time he had his head tipped down, watching her. Surprised, she almost dropped her head again, but didn't.

"I'm always going to ask things you don't want to answer," she said.

"I know."

"And?"

"And what? I'll be silent or say something douchey. You know I will," he said.

She smiled. That element of honesty mixed with

self-deprecation never failed to make her like him even more. He might be warning her, but he never delivered on the darkness he cautioned her against. Her heart was telling her that was because he was an inherently good man worthy of her affection. But her mind was a little more cynical and wary of being hurt again. In the short time they'd known each other, she'd been more real with him than she had been with anyone in Gilbert Corners, including Nola.

"I do know. You know me too. Why are we both so honest with each other?" she asked.

"Because we know this won't last."

She stiffened with shock at his words. But then they settled in; she'd said as much to herself. He was right. They both knew it. It made her sad to hear it out loud, but as he'd said, he wasn't one to lie. And neither was she. As much as she might have pretended to want to hear something that would soften the truth, she'd have seen through it and been upset if he'd lied to her.

"I know. I wish..."

She trailed off. What did she wish? There was nothing she could say that would be true.

"I wish too," he said, gruffly. "But for now, let's take this day and pretend that we both aren't realists."

She thought about it for a few moments. Could she do that? Why not? As he said, they both weren't going to pretend this was the prelude to forever. They both knew that their lives weren't going to merge together suddenly and magically. Today was a moment they'd have to look back on. Fondly, she promised herself.

"No regrets."

"Never with you, lady," he said, rolling them to their sides as he pulled away from her. "I'll go shower in another room and meet you back in the kitchen."

She shook her head. "Shower with me. This day isn't going to last forever, and I don't want to waste a minute of it without you."

He nodded in that short way of his. Then sat up and got to his feet before reaching back and lifting her in his arms. "No one's ever carried me before."

He arched one eyebrow at her. "Like it?"

"I do. Makes me feel like a princess," she said.

"Hmm. Too bad you don't have a white knight."

"I do. I have you."

"I'm not a white knight."

"Today you are," she said. She wished they had more than this time together. So she could show him the man she saw behind the thorns that he'd wrapped himself in. Behind the legend and the temper he used to keep everyone at bay. But she didn't, so she'd just push and take what she needed from him while he was here in her arms.

"Today only."

"That's all I need," she said but even as the words left her mouth, she knew they were a lie. She'd prided herself on being truthful, but she couldn't be now. She only had one day with Conrad and she wasn't going to ruin it with the truth.

Twelve

Indy had given up on trying to cook and sat on a stool watching him making pasta, talking about her favorite books. It was as if, by saying they only had this one day, he'd unlocked something in her.

"So what's the book about again?" he asked. She was trying to explain the plot of *A Swiftly Tilting Planet*, the third book in the Madeleine L'Engle *A Wrinkle in Time* series. Which he'd read when he'd been a teenager. He and Dash had read it when Rory did because she liked talking about books. He had a feeling that Rory and Indy would get along great. Or the Rory he had known. She was of course a shadow of the girl he'd known now.

But there was a real woman sitting there talking to him about her dreams and her love of fairy tales and books; it gave him hope that Rory might find that one day. He thought of the trauma from Indy's past that she'd dealt with. God, she was such a strong person. At times he was in awe of that strength in her because it allowed her to be open.

His strength was a fortress he used to keep everyone at bay. Hers was a warm hearth inviting those she chose to come closer and be comforted by it.

He wasn't sure he was worthy of being invited in. God, when was he going to? Today when he was with this woman, who had turned him inside out, he had wanted to celebrate so much of himself—and he still couldn't just exhale and let himself be with her.

She took a deep breath. "I love the sibling dynamics in the book. I'm an only child."

"As am I," he said. "But as you know I was raised with Rory and Dash, so I'm sort of not. I read that series a long time ago. It was okay. If you want a really good science fiction book, you should try *Dune*."

"I have. Oh my gosh, it makes my head hurt when I read it. I have to pay close attention to everything. I really like a book I can just sink into and not have to...well, think so much," she said. "What about you?"

"I don't read that much anymore. I will sometimes put an audio book on when I go for a ride on the bike," he said.

She shook her head, smiling at him.

"What?"

"I'm just picturing you looking like a badass on your bike and listening to *Dune*."

He laughed softly. “I can see your point. What’s the best book you’ve read lately?”

“Hmm…not sure I can pick just one. My go-to is always historical romance.”

He hadn’t heard of the genre. “What do you love about it?”

She tipped her head to the side, chewing her lower lip which he noticed she did when she was weighing her words. “Part of what I like is just the setting, usually in Regency England, and the lavish balls and all the manors of that time. But the other part is the romance. I mean who doesn’t love falling in love.”

“Me.”

She arched both eyebrows at him. “Is that true?”

“Maybe.” To be honest he’d never really thought about love. His adult life he hadn’t allowed himself to ever love anyone. But what he’d absorbed from watching others had convinced him that love seemed like the worst sort of emotion. He’d loved his parents and had felt so lost after their deaths.

He’d been in love with himself for his early adult years, thinking he was the only one who mattered until that horrible night with the fight and the crash. After that he’d pumped the brakes. Of course he’d had to. His recovery had taken all of his strength and when he was done, love had been the last thing he’d wanted to find.

“Why?” she asked.

He looked at the workbench where he’d cut the pasta into long strips of tagliatelle, pretending he had to flour them again, but the truth was he found this hard to talk about. Sure, in his head it made a sort of sense. But this wasn't something he'd ever say to anyone. Not even Dash.

"It's okay to tell me, as you said, this is probably the last time we'll be together this way," she said.

"I'm not sure I can. Life just feels saner without love. Even you have to admit that."

"How do you figure?"

"Well, you're here with me, for one, and you had been hibernating in Gilbert Corners before," he pointed out.

"I wasn't hibernating. And just because I'm not out there actively looking for love doesn't mean I don't want to find it someday."

"Someday?"

"Yes. I don't know when it will happen. Just like you don't know that it won't happen," she said.

"I can't imagine falling in love with anyone."

"Why not? Do you think no one can live up to your expectations?"

"Not at all," he said, realizing that Indy would probably come close to any expectation he had for a life partner. "It's more that I can't imagine letting myself be that vulnerable to another person."

She got off her stool and came around the counter to him. She put her arms around his waist and hugged him from behind.

"Oh, Conrad."

He stood there not sure what he'd done to elicit that reaction or even how he was supposed to respond.

He liked the feeling of her pressed along his back

and he wanted her again, but he was already too deeply in like with her. He had to start pulling back, so he contented himself with a pat of her joined hands and then turned, breaking her hug.

"Oh, what?"

She chewed her lower lip and looked up at him until their eyes met and she sighed. "You try so hard to keep everything inside, but you can't."

"What do you mean try?"

She shrugged. "You won't like what I have to say."

"As you pointed out, we're not hanging out after today," he said.

"Fine. You have covered your body in thorny tattoos as if in some way those will keep people from getting closer to you or keep you from letting them close, but you reach out to everyone around you all the time."

"How?" he asked.

"With food. You picked a career in the one area that creates a connection between you and everyone. Food is love—everyone knows that. It's just that you cook for strangers so you can control the love. It's not that you don't love love. It's that you're afraid of it."

Indy knew she was pushing him, but it was hard not to. She'd been sitting there watching him cook and realized what she'd known deep in her soul all along. She didn't want this to be their only time together like this. She wasn't someone who needed a man in her life, not that there was anything wrong with that. She'd just always been fiercely independent and shy. And after her assault, she'd gone even deeper into herself.

But she had also found people along the way who she resonated with, and Conrad was a man she *definitely* resonated with. She thought maybe it was because he was so locked away in his thorny vest trying to keep the world at bay with his roar that she was drawn to him.

In her quiet way she did the same thing. But she used a book in her hands to do it.

She watched his face go stony as he brought his arms up to his hips, glaring at her. She might have gone too far.

Who wanted to have their fears pointed out?

"Afraid?"

She was tempted to backpedal. It would be the easiest way to get out of this, except she didn't want out. She needed to know what it was that kept him from wanting more intimacy, because maybe it would help her figure out why the only person she'd taken a chance on was a man who didn't want it.

She knew she was pointing out something in Conrad that she herself felt. Something she didn't want to cop to. He was just blunt enough to maybe give her some insight or…or say something that would hopefully make her stop seeing him in this light. This romantic light that made her believe she could help him. Even though she was pretty sure he didn't want to be helped, and that she didn't have the skills to do it.

"Yup. That's what I said. Listen, there's nothing wrong with being afraid of love," she said.

"Thanks," he said sarcastically. "I guess that's your own fear talking right?"

"You're deflecting," she said.

"You are too."

She leaned back against the wall behind her. "I am. I just… I wish there was some way we could both somehow be different but the same. I sort of want everything to be different so we could have more time together. Like this."

That seemed to relax him. She thought she could see the tension leave his body, and he came closer to her. Reaching out, he stroked the side of her face in a way that almost made her believe he returned her feelings. But then, she already knew he liked her. And liking wasn't enough. Liking wasn't what she was after.

She knew that it wasn't her—Indy Belmont—he objected to as much as it was his fear of being hurt. Though she suspected he wouldn't say it that way.

"Just let this be enough," he said. "I'm really not good at anything long-term. Not even the restaurant."

Not good at long term.

Didn't love love.

He was telling her these things to keep her from getting hurt. To keep her from doing something impulsive and passionate and making a mistake that she'd end up regretting.

"Me either," she said.

"Liar," he countered but not unkindly. "You might

want to be, but everything about you and this move to Gilbert Corners says otherwise."

"I don't see that," she said.

"You're trying to break the town curse. You want to bring business to the town—you are fixing it in a way that I think you want to fix me."

She chewed her lower lip. "I didn't say that."

"You didn't have to," he said. "I know I need fixing. I'm not trying to pretend that I don't. That's why I don't do this."

He gestured to the two of them and she got it. He'd said he wasn't into dating.

"So why are you?" she asked.

He shrugged and looked away then turned back to the counter where he had been making pasta. She was pretty sure he either wasn't going to answer or was trying to come up with a falsehood she'd believe. She took a deep breath and knew she could save him by just saying something glib and changing the subject and she almost did.

Almost.

But then she saw the thorny branch that came up from the back of his neck, above the fabric of his shirt, and wrapped around his shoulder just the tiniest bit, and knew she couldn't. She wanted to be the princess who ripped down the thorns and found her way to the prince waiting inside.

"You like me," she said. "You might not want to. You might wish it was just lust and getting laid but it's more than that."

"You're right, I do wish you were like every other

woman I've screwed, but you're not. I think that's why I'm hesitating here, which isn't like me. I'm talking about bringing my show and maybe a restaurant to Gilbert Corners, but I'm keeping it from you."

"Why?"

He put his head down and she saw him struggling for the words. It was easier to smash things, she thought, easier to fight than to talk things through. But she needed to know. "Is it because you don't care?" she asked.

He didn't say anything, and she walked around the island and leaned on the other side of the counter. He looked up and she saw some unfathomable emotion pass over his features. For a second it looked like hope and regret mixed together.

"Did you get that from reading a book in your bookshop where you hide from the world?"

She knew he was trying to rile her, but this was too important to let anger come into play. "No. I got that from talking to you. From riding behind you on your bike and walking through this ghost-filled home of your childhood. You might think you are keeping your emotions locked away but you're not. Not to me anyway. I see you."

He put both hands flat on the counter and leaned over so that only a few inches separated them. "You see what you want to see."

No one had gotten under his skin the way that Indy was today. He hated it, and yet at the same time a part of him enjoyed it. He was afraid to admit too much to her, but he had been alone for so long he'd sort of thought life was better that way. But with Indy…it wasn't. She'd awakened something in him that he wanted to explore, but it was becoming increasingly obvious that he couldn't control her or her responses.

Why couldn't she just eat pasta and make love to him again and let this day be a happy memory?

Probably for the same reason that he was trying to make it into one. Both of them were seeing in the other what they needed. Not what the other one did. He needed this one day of happy memories in the place that still haunted him, and she needed a lifetime of happy memories to replace the date that had stolen her innocence from her.

"I see you," she said. "But I'll stop pushing, if you come to town and build your restaurant. I'll keep my distance. I know what it's like to be confronted every day with someone you don't want to see."

She stepped back and went to her stool, sat down on it.

He wanted to be a different man. Wanted to give her this thing she thought she wanted with him. Even though he knew if he did, he'd hurt her. He'd disappoint her and become a regret. This wasn't him guessing or trying to make himself feel better. He wasn't into lying to himself even when it would be easier.

He was difficult and hard to be around. Even Dash had said so, and Dash was the one person on the planet who truly knew him.

"I want to see you. I don't want to hurt you," the words were torn from somewhere deep inside him. A place that he wasn't sure he wanted to acknowledge he had.

"I know."

Those quiet words tore him apart.

"There. You see it too."

She shook her head. "I see us. We have both been pushed past limits that would have broken others, but instead we both took those scars and the pain and made ourselves stronger. I know you need someone who can be light and make you laugh—"

"You do that."

"Until I get like this," she said.

He wasn't sure what she was getting at. "Oh, lady, this is a Conrad problem, not an Indy one."

She shook her head. "Nothing is all your fault. I want to take a chance on us. And I know we had sex and have had what, one and a half dates. So there isn't really an us, but I feel like maybe there could be. I guess…well all of this is me trying to ask you to take a chance too."

Take a chance.

No one had ever said those words to him. He had simply just always done what he wanted and dragged people along with him in his career and he had no real personal life. Could he do what she was asking?

Sure. Of course he could. But could he do it and not hurt her or get hurt himself in the process? Because he wasn't sure he could handle letting down another woman he cared about.

And there were no two ways about that. He had let Rory down, and the consequences had left her in coma. He knew he hadn't been driving, hadn't caused the accident, but that didn't change the fact that he'd exacerbated an already tense situation and made it harder for his cousin.

"Conrad?"

He was taking too long to respond. But he didn't know if he could. How was he going to do this? Since he'd woken up in that hospital bed nearly ten years ago, his life had been about learning to live with the pain, then relearning to walk, then figuring out how to cope with life, then the restaurant, then TV. All solitary prospects, but she wanted him to agree to something else. To try something with her.

"Forget it. So what do we need to do for the rest of this dish? Make some kind of sauce?"

She got up and came around by him. He closed his eyes as the scent of summer flowers surrounded him. She was so close. She wasn't asking him to be perfect or expecting him to meet her needs. He could reach out and take her in his arms and to his bed again. She wouldn't' deny him.

But he'd disappoint her. He'd already done that.

His heart started beating so loudly he could hear it in his ears and he'd be surprised if she couldn't hear it. Fear.

She'd called him on it and she was right.

"I don't want to hurt you."

"I know—it's cool. Forget I—"

"I can't. I can't forget you said it. I hate disappointing you," he said. The rest of the words were stuck in his throat.

"You're not. I pushed. I do that when I care about someone. I can't promise I won't do it again. You set boundaries, I agreed to them and then I decided I wanted more, not your fault."

He pulled her into his arms and brought his mouth down hard on hers. He held her to him closely; there was nothing tentative about the emotions she stirred inside him, and he tried to show her all the things that he knew he couldn't' say with his kisses. He pushed his tongue deeper into her mouth, and she wrapped her arms around him and clung to him as if she'd never let him go.

The storm of emotions ebbed, leaving him feeling like a battered boardwalk and seashore after a hurricane, still standing but just. Still holding the woman he wanted in his arms. He looked down into her face and realized, like that midnight call he'd made to her, he wasn't going to be able to just limit himself to one day with her.

No matter what he'd said or how smart that would be.

"I'd like to try to see you again."

The words sounded rusty and slow in his head, but she heard them. She touched the side of his face, and he knew that no amount of thorny branches tattooed around his body was going to keep him safe. She was already inching her way in and he had no idea what to do with her.

Thirteen

Indy hadn't really thought through what seeing him again would entail. Dating hadn't been something either of them were regulars at. Their dates had become something unexpected, she thought as she saw him standing in the doorway outside her shop a week later. She'd finished a long day filming over at the deli and then stopped by the shop because it helped her relax to be surrounded by books.

Conrad wore a navy blue suit that made his eyes pop. He had on a dress shirt with no tie, and she could see those thorny tattoos around his lower neck as she finished putting away her stuff for the day and walked toward him.

"Are you sure about this? If the people of Gilbert

Corners think I'm cursed, I probably shouldn't be seen here," he said.

"Oh, I'm sure, plus it sounds like fun. Why are you wearing a modern suit? I told you to dress in 1920s' garb."

"I figured I'd leave that to you, doll," he said, pulling her into his arms and kissing her. His kiss swept her away from everything, turning her on and making her want to skip the secret pop-up speakeasy that had opened. She suspected that was why he'd kissed her.

She pulled back, brushing her hands down the flapper-inspired beaded dress she wore, winked at him and said, "Thanks, doll."

He laughed and double-checked the door after she locked it. "So where is this place?"

"That's part of the fun—we have to unravel the clues to find it," she said, taking out her phone and going to the Gilbert Corners app.

"You're on the Main Street Business Alliance—don't you know where it is?" he asked.

"Uh, maybe," she said. She did know because all of the businesses around the town square had chipped in to open the pop-up. But she also wanted to see if they could figure out the clues. This was the first night of the club. Social media influencers and dignitaries from other neighboring towns had been invited as well.

"Good thing I recruited some help," he said, lifting his hand and waving someone over.

She turned to see who it was. She was pretty sure

it was his cousin Dash Gilbert, whom she'd never met but had seen a photo of on his company's website. He wore a suit similar to the one Conrad had on, but he didn't look as sexy in it.

"Hello," she said as he joined them.

"Hi. I'm Dash," he said offering his hand.

"Indy," she said. "So we have to follow the clues to find the speakeasy."

"Yeah, the head of the committee doesn't know where it is," Conrad said.

She turned and lightly mock punched his arm. "It's supposed to be secret."

"What's the first clue?" Conrad asked.

"Gluten-free or full fat, this is the place to get your baked goods and start your journey," she read out loud.

"Java Juice. Nola Weston owns it," Conrad said. "Let's go."

"Nola? I think she was friends with Rory?" Dash asked.

"She is. She's my best friend and works on my TV show with me as well," Indy said.

"I hadn't made that connection before this," Dash said. "I can't wait to see her again."

The cousins talked back and forth while Indy looked at her phone and noticed a typo on the next clue, which she jotted down on a feedback page for the committee in her notes app. The map was taking them all around the square and then to the back of the old milliner's shop, which had been out of use since the 1970s and was the easiest to get up to building code and open as a bar.

Conrad noticed she was walking behind him and his cousin and stopped to take her hand so that they were walking together. Dash noticed the gesture and then noticed her noticing and winked at her. She smiled back, taking that as a good sign.

Conrad's tattoos weren't the only thing thorny; he was too. It seemed each date they went on started slow, like they were both trying to figure out what to do. He always pushed her sexually, and not in an uncomfortable way; she loved making love with him, but she had the feeling he was trying to make every encounter between them sexual and she wanted—no, needed—more than that. From his own admission most of his "relationships" in the past had been sexual in nature, and she had a feeling after they'd talked about everything that he had done that to protect himself.

Because she knew she was falling for him, she had to coax him out even though just staying home and making love was one of her favorite ways to spend time with him. Tonight it was as if he'd anticipated it and brought his cousin along.

They followed the clues which lead them along the town square.

"I really like to see the town coming back to life," Dash said. "The council members have done a good job with the park and the business here on Main Street."

"They needed a nudge, but once I convinced them

there was a way to break the curse, they got on board," she said.

"By bringing Conrad back here?" Dash asked.

"That's right. Seems I'm the most important Gilbert."

"Well, you were the easiest to get here," Indy said.

Dash started laughing.

"I'm not easy."

"No, you're not."

"Glad you agree. So me coming to town made them think the curse is broken?" Conrad asked her as they got closer to the speakeasy.

"Sort of. They are more inclined to think of it as a thaw. Until we get the factory open and all the businesses on Main Street open again, I'm not sure the curse will be lifted," she said.

"Dash and I are working on the factory in addition to the restaurant space I mentioned," Conrad said.

"What else are you doing there?" she asked. She was surprised and a little hurt that he never mentioned it to her. She'd heard gossip around town of course but she would have liked to have heard it from him. As much as he'd opened up to her, there were still things he kept hidden behind his thorny branches.

"A television studio, which I want to talk to you about. Might be nice to have a production studio here," Conrad said. "In fact, I was planning to talk to you about it tonight before we went on this date."

"I'd love to discuss that more in depth," she told him. Well, that wasn't what she'd expected. He wasn't running away after all. Did this mean he wanted something more permanent?

"I think this is the place," she said. "The password is *Gilbert's a goose*."

"Really?"

"Yes. I know it needs work, but we were out of ideas," she said.

The bouncer let them in, and they weren't the first to arrive. The bar was toward the back and the interior was decorated as a 1920s' club with a dance floor in the middle and a stage at the end where they had a chanteuse singing. Dash volunteered to go to the bar and get drinks for them while she and Conrad found a table.

"So you brought your cousin on our date?" she asked. "Not sure if that's a good sign or not."

"I knew you'd say no to staying in and getting naked with me," he said with a wink. "I wanted Dash to see what you've been doing here in town."

"Why?"

"Because I'm proud of your hard work," he said, then leaned over to kiss her.

She felt a spark go through her and her heart beat faster as her mind was starting to think that pushing for this closeness was going to pay off.

Conrad wasn't sure how he found himself watching his cousin and Indy dance and getting slightly jealous, even though after two absinthe cocktails, Indy had told him that there wasn't a man alive who looked as good as he did in a suit. He knew she wasn't into anyone but him.

Which made him happier than it should have. The plain fact of the matter was the more time he spent with her, the more he realized that there was no way to keep her at arm's length. He had thought that agreeing to this dating thing would potentially bore him and that he'd grow tired of her.

But he hadn't. He was catching feelings and they were strong. Stronger than anything he experienced before and a part of him wanted to growl about it. But when he looked at Indy he just…well he couldn't growl. She made him feel good inside and as much as he'd struggled with believing he deserved this kind of happiness he felt it was right there if he only had the courage to reach out and take it.

"Why aren't you dancing?" Nola asked sitting down next to him. Nola was dressed like a gangster tonight in a pair of wide-leg dark pants with suspenders and a white shirt. She had on a flak cap and her hair had been pulled back to a low bun at the nape of her neck.

"Why aren't you?"

"I have no coordination and the Charleston requires too much thinking."

"Same."

"I doubt that."

"Dash asked Indy and we can't both dance with her," he said.

"So noble."

"That's me."

"Your reputation says otherwise."

He arched both eyebrows at her. "Is there a reason for this?"

She shrugged. "Indy is one of my few friends. I don't want to see her get hurt. That being said, I'm glad to see the Gilberts back in town."

He didn't want to hurt her either. He hoped he wouldn't. "The town is starting to shape up."

"Thanks to your girl."

His girl.

Was he ready for this? Date by date he had been letting her into his life and there were times when he held back because he was afraid. But the truth was, for weeks now he knew that he wanted more from Indy, and from himself.

Neither of them was good at dating, and sitting in a restaurant or going to a movie didn't appeal to them. So they'd had a picnic at his place in the city. Another night Indy insisted they lie on her couch and he read out loud to her from a book of poems by Lord Byron. Then there was tonight, the speakeasy around Gilbert Corners. Two people who were both used to the spotlight when it came to their TV shows guarding their privacy just letting their guards down with each other.

It felt odd to have found a woman who suited him so perfectly. It made him remember the man he'd been before the accident and he didn't necessarily like it. She was putting him in touch with parts of himself he'd ignored for a long time. He didn't know how to move forward. But he sensed that was fear holding him back.

"Indy's thc best," he said, but even to his own ears that sounded trite. She was so much more than the best. She'd put her heart and soul into rejuvenating this town. And next weekend he was going to come to town with his TV show and give her the national exposure she wanted.

"She is. So your show taping…do you need any audience members?" Nola asked. "My mom is a huge fan."

He had the feeling this was really why Nola was over here. "I'll put you in touch with my producer. Give me your number."

She pulled a business card out of her pocket and handed it to him. "Thanks. I'm going to ask your cousin to dance so Indy will be free."

He got to his feet but didn't follow Nola. The last time he'd danced with anyone had been that winter ball ten years ago.

The thought had sort of drifted in from nowhere. Maybe it was being back in this place and seeing so many familiar faces all drinking and dancing that was stirring up old memories. Or maybe it was Indy who was nudging him to get some closure with his past. He needed to get out of here and get some air.

But as he turned to go, Indy caught his arm. "Dance with me. Just one dance. We can stand in the corner and sway together if you don't know the steps. I just want to be in your arms."

She looked up at him, her eyes wide and shining

with that deep affection that he knew was that emotion…the L-word. The one he didn't believe in and certainly didn't want to see on her face. The one that should have been the impetus for him to turn on his heel and walk away but instead he just nodded.

He wouldn't deny her tonight. She wanted to be in his arms, and he wanted her there. The music was that old standard a bit later than the 1920s "The Very Thought of You," and he pulled her into his arms without thinking of the consequences.

He should have stuck to his guns that day at the mansion; he had known it then, and tonight it was confirmed. He wasn't going to indulge himself and his emotions. He knew how dangerous that could be and he had to end this.

But not tonight, as Indy was in his arms, singing off-key and messing up the lyrics while her hand stroked along with the drumbeat at the back of his neck. He held her closer and knew that he might have never believed in this kind of relationship, but the truth was, he'd feared it. Had remembered the closeness of his parents, the way his grandfather had been so cold and angry after Conrad's grandmother's death.

He'd never wanted to admit he had anything in common with the old man, but had his grandfather kept everyone at arm's length to protect them? Fuck. He really didn't like the path his thoughts were taking. But his gut told him that walking away from Indy was going to be the only way he could keep from following that path that led to anger. Anger had always been the emotion that had ruled him and essentially driven his success. He felt himself falling for her. He'd never let himself be this open or vulnerable to another person, and he was afraid that he'd turn into a true beast if he lost her. Nothing could ever fill the emptiness he felt at the thought of not having Indy by his side and in his arms.

The stars looked close enough to touch as Conrad held her hand and walked her home. "The speakeasy was a big hit. Don't you think?"

"Yeah. Everyone seemed to like it," he said.

She glanced over at him; she was a bit tipsy, but not too much. "Not your scene?"

"Not really."

She could see that. He wasn't someone for going out. "It's funny that you've always been in the spotlight but hate it so much."

"I don't think that's funny at all. It's probably because I've always been in it that I don't like it."

"True. So why become a TV chef?"

"I didn't mean to. My producer and partner in the restaurant suggested it after I stepped back from being there full-time. It just sort of happened," he said.

"You are so not a sort-of-happened kind of man," she said.

"You're right. I might hate the spotlight, but I also hate the idea of not being in it," he admitted. "I'm sure you're not shocked that I have a huge ego."

She shook her head. "I'm not, but you're not a humblebrag kind of guy. I think you like success and the kudos that come with it, but is it that you are trying to prove something to yourself…or your grandfather?"

When she'd been dancing with Dash, he'd mentioned that he had rarely enjoyed being in Gilbert Corners, which had added to what Conrad had said about their grandfather. She was glad she'd never met him; he sounded like he must have been difficult.

"Yeah."

That was probably as much of an answer as he was going to give, and she wasn't going to push him for more. Not tonight. Not when the stars were bright and she had Conrad by her side.

She knew she was falling for him. It had been there all the time, but she'd ignored it until tonight when he'd taken her hand and pulled her to his side. She hadn't realized that she'd been searching for—someone to walk by her side. Someone who she could trust enough to be this public with and this intimate with.

But now that she knew it, she couldn't go back from it.

"I saw you talking to Nola."

"She wants to provide coffee and snacks for the TV crew when we come to town, and also doesn't want you to get hurt."

"No one can hurt me," she said.

"Good."

But she knew that wasn't true. She could hurt herself by seeing something in Conrad that might not be there. It was one thing to tell herself that he was starting to come out of his thorny cave, but it was something else for him to do it. Was she actually seeing glimpses of the real man, or was she just making any small gesture seem like it?

Who was he really?

She knew he wasn't a man who liked to fail. Was that why he was here with her? He knew he had nothing to worry about in the kitchen when it came to her. But maybe her challenging him at the mansion had made him want to prove something.

"We haven't really checked in on the dating thing," she said, abruptly.

God, when was she going to have a thought and keep it to herself?

He arched both eyebrows at her the way he did sometimes.

"Well?"

"That wasn't a question, lady," he said.

A little of the tension she was carrying disappeared when he called her lady in that soft tone he used only when they were alone.

"Do you think it's working?" she asked.

"Do you?"

"Ugh."

"Ugh?"

"Conrad, stop doing that. I'm being serious."

He stopped walking and pulled her into his arms. "I know."

She put her arms around his neck and looked up at him. He was a big man with a muscly body who didn't need anyone to protect him, and yet there were moments like this when she saw a flash of vulnerability and she wanted to defend him.

"So?"

"Do we have to discuss this?" he asked.

"I guess not. Did I force you to date me?"

He started laughing and lifted her off her feet. "Lady, you couldn't force me to do anything. I'm here because I want to be here."

Those words put her mind at ease and she wrapped her arms around him and kissed him as he held her. Not the little sweet kisses they'd shared through the night but a deep, passionate kiss, because she was very aware that he hadn't answered her question and that there was a panic building inside her as she fell harder for him.

Was this going to last?

She'd been okay on her own, had planned out a life for herself where she accepted who she was and what was enough. Then Conrad came into it. To be fair, she'd drawn him here.

But all the same, this man who she was kissing with the kind of passion she thought she'd never experience again had changed something in her. Had made her start to dream of a future again and she didn't want to give it up.

And the harder she worked to make sure he felt safe and not chained to her, the more she wanted to wrap him in them as a couple. The more she felt compelled to make him see that they were stronger as a couple. The more she wanted to find a way to make him stay by her side.

Or force him to tell her that he couldn't. She knew that love took time, that she needed to be patient and let things unfold as they were meant to. But she wasn't sure she could do that.

She loved him. She had been trying not to, but she did. And Conrad was… Conrad. She felt that deep well of caring inside him, but he'd had a decade of being on his own and had gotten so used to not caring that she feared if she didn't push him to admit his feelings, he never would.

She'd risked everything on Conrad Gilbert, and she hadn't meant to.

He set her on her feet and they finished the walk to her house in silence. Her mind was buzzing with questions and the need for answers and her body was buzzing for him.

Of the two, she chose the safer option and led him up the stairs to her bed.

Fourteen

Conrad leaned against the wall in the hall outside her bedroom. He didn't want to be in her bed again. He needed to claim her but they were becoming too comfortable. Too much like a real couple. Tonight…well, tonight had been the moment where he had to face himself and admit that he'd let this go on too long.

He pulled her against him, so that her breasts rested against his chest and her hips were nestled against him. She leaned up on her tiptoes, her hands on his shoulders, and he put his hands under her butt and lifted her up so they could see each other eye to eye. Hers were still a bit bloodshot from the drinks earlier, but he saw the seriousness in them. Knew that they both didn't have to say it out loud but were thinking the same thing.

This had to end. He saw what she wanted from him; he wanted it too. But there was too much potential for it to go wrong. For him to actually earn the Beast moniker. Not toward her, but if anything happened to her…it was a chance he just didn't think he could take.

They weren't going to find a way to some sort of Hollywood version of happily-ever-after. That had never been the kind of man he was.

She opened her mouth to speak, but he wanted this last night, this time with her in his arms so he brought his mouth down on hers. Angled his head so that he could kiss her slowly and deeply. He took his time wanting this kiss to be enough to keep him satiated for the rest of his life. Even though he knew one kiss would never be enough.

Her hands moved up his shoulders, her fingers pushing into his hair as her tongue rubbed over his, and then she sucked his tongue deeper into her mouth. She tasted of absinthe and that extra special flavor that he had only tasted when he kissed her. He'd tried to re-create her in a dish, but it wasn't possible.

These feelings that stirred in him when she was in his arms came only from Indy. There was no way to replicate it on the plate or in his life. He knew that.

Fuck.

He turned so that she was between him and the wall before he realized what he was doing and started to step back.

"Sorry. I didn't mean to trap you."

She put her hand on the side of his face, rubbing her finger along his jawline. "I don't feel trapped with you. It's okay."

Those words made him feel—fuck, he wasn't able to think of anything but white-hot passion. He shut down the other thoughts in his head. Hell, he was going to get his rocks off…except when had making love with Indy been about just a long, hard orgasm? It hadn't. It couldn't be. Indy was too deeply embedded in him for sex to be just getting laid.

Which should have been a red flag from the very beginning, but in his arrogance, he'd thought he could control it. Hell, he *was* controlling it.

He brought his mouth down on hers again as his hands swept down her, finding the hem of her flapper dress and then pulling it up her body where it got wedged between the two of them and he left it there, as he could feel the bare skin at the tops of her thighs. He swept his fingers higher to her panties, before pushing them underneath and then slowly sliding the underwear down her legs. He didn't bother tossing it to the floor, just left it at her knees so he could caress her nakedness.

She shifted back and forth, and he realized she was working her panties down her legs as he took one full cheek of her butt in his hands, running his finger along her crack as he deepened the kiss even more. He was hungry for her as if it had been years instead of days since he'd had her.

His erection was full, straining against the zipper of his pants, and he knew if he freed himself he'd be inside her, and he wanted this last time to take forever. He wanted to draw out the passion. So he pulled his hips back and dropped to his knees between her legs. The scent of her arousal enflamed him and made him harder.

His blood felt like molten lava as it flowed through his body. Her hands were in his hair as he parted her nether lips, revealing her clit. He breathed on it, then licked her. She moaned and her hands tightened in his hair.

He opened his eyes, trying to memorize everything about her in this moment. The dark curly hair that protected her femininity. The birthmark at the top of her left thigh right where her pubic area began. The way her hands lifted from his head and then landed again as he drove her higher and higher.

He drowned all of his senses in Indy. He let every part of her essence sink into his mind. He listened carefully to her breathing and the tiny moans she made, the sounds getting closer and closer to the moment when he knew she'd orgasm.

His own body was on fire, and it was only the fact that he'd had a lifetime of keeping himself in check that he could wait. He wanted this. He liked when she came before him. Liked tasting the passion in her and then driving her wild again in his arms.

Tonight though, it was more poignant, as this was the last time he'd taste her like this. The last time he'd hear her voice getting deeper and her sighs turning into longer moans until her legs flexed as her hips drove forward and she tunneled her fingers into his hair holding him to her as she cried out his name and came in his arms.

He looked up her body, craning his head so he could see her arched against the wall in ecstasy and he knew he'd never forget this moment or this woman. But for the sake of both of their souls he had to leave her after this and never come back.

The energy coming off Conrad was intense, and she couldn't read anything but the lust and desire… but she knew there was more. Something had changed between them. She knew that he must feel it too. If only she still believed in fairy tales, then she would tell herself that this was the beginning of forever.

But she lived in the real world where their past baggage didn't easily disappear, and sometimes the emotional wounds of childhood couldn't be cured with a new love. She slid down the wall, crouching in front of him. He looked at her but he didn't speak, and she could tell from the look on his face that he was in sex mode. She'd seen that passionate intensity too many times to mistake it for anything else.

She reached for the buttons of his shirt and her fingers fumbled with them, making it hard to undo them. The emotions of this moment, the feeling that this might be the last time she was alone with him like this overwhelmed her, and she cursed under her breath before she took the two sides of the shirt and pulled until the buttons burst and his shirt fell open.

She didn't look at him as she pushed her hands into the opening, tried to ignore those thorny branches that encased his torso, feeling the ridges of those old scars. But she couldn't ignore any of it. These were the things that made Conrad the man he was. Made him the man she liked—when was she going to feel comfortable with this admission. The man she loved.

Since he was making love to her like it was the last time, she wanted this. Wanted to admit to herself that she loved him and take this moment and make it into everything she'd ever secretly wanted and always believed she couldn't have.

His pectorals flexed as she ran her fingernail over his left nipple and then down the side of his body. She leaned in closer, biting his nipple and then licking it before following the path her finger hand taken with her mouth.

She took her time over the ridged indentation of his abdomen and then lower where that thin line of hair led to his cock. She saw his erection pressing against the fabric of his trousers and it made her hotter and wetter than his mouth had. She reached down to stroke him through his pants. Then she found the tab of his zipper and started to lower it, but he brushed her hands aside, did it himself. He stood and she frowned at him until he took off his pants and underwear and then sank back down on the floor against the wall.

"Shirts are easier to replace than pants," he said.

She smiled at him. "I'll buy you a new one."

"No need. Just climb on top of me and make love to me, Indy."

He had never called her by her name when they were intimate, and she had the feeling he only did so now because he was planning for this to be the last time. She could just feel it in the air around them.

"Oh, I plan to, Conrad."

He pushed his hands into her hair, jostling the pins she'd used to hold it in the Gibson Girl hairstyle and then his big hand rubbed against the back of her head as he pulled her face toward his. Their lips met and their kiss was deep and intense as she straddled him. She felt the ridge of his erection between her legs and she shifted her hips back and forth to ride it.

He felt so good as his big fingers moved over her intimate flesh. He shifted under her. His hands on her waist lifting her and then his mouth found her breast, suckled at her nipple as he positioned her so that his cock was poised to enter her. She put her hands on his shoulders, looking down at him. His head at her breast, his cock at her entrance, his scared and beautiful body underneath her.

She couldn't breathe from want. Both the physical desire for him and the emotional craving. But then his hands moved to her butt, one finger running along her crack, making her shiver and forget about everything but getting him inside her.

Slowly she lowered herself on him until he was

fully seated in her body. He was so big that it always took her a moment to adjust to having him inside her. He lifted his head from her breast and their eyes met and she opened her mouth to say his name. He tangled his hand in her loose hair and drew her head to his shoulder, his mouth finding that spot where the base of her neck met her shoulder and then sucking on her skin as he moved underneath. He drove himself up into her and she moved on him. He held her to him, and they felt like one as they found their rhythm.

She felt her climax building and wanted to prolong it, but it felt too good. *He* felt too good as he moved faster and faster under her and then rolled them over so she was underneath him. Their eyes met and she wrapped her arms and legs around him as he drove even deeper, and she came. Shivers wracked her body and stars danced around her as she cried out his name. He drove into her a few more times before he emptied himself in her and called her name too.

He held his weight off her as he lowered his head, resting it against her breast as the sweat dried on their bodies. She put her arms around him and whispered in her mind the truth that she was no longer denying to herself.

I love you.

She had never thought until this moment that love couldn't make everything okay.

Conrad pushed himself to his feet and offered his hand to Indy. He'd been surprised when she'd ripped his shirt off but he'd liked it. She suited him on even levels that he hadn't revealed to her. She chewed her lower lip as she gathered her clothes off the floor. "Are you staying?"

"Yes."

He had promised himself tonight and he was going to take it. "I could use a shower. Want to join me?"

"How about if we share a bath?" she asked. There was almost a fragility to her as she stood there clutching her dress to her chest.

He didn't remember taking it from her body. Just that need to get her naked in his arms.

"Okay. Let's do it."

She walked into her bedroom and tossed her clothes to the floor as she continued to the bathroom; he tossed his near hers. He had an extra set of clothes stored in his bike. Which he'd get in the morning. He wanted this night to be just everything that day at the mansion had started out as.

That part of him that feared love and the ties that it brought made him want to leave right now. While she was in there running the bath. But that was the coward's way out and he wasn't one.

He also wouldn't do that to her. When he left in the morning, she'd know that he wasn't coming back except to fulfill his promises to Gilbert Corners. Damn, there were times when he hated himself.

It had been a long time since he had. He stood in the doorway and watched her staring at the tub that was filling with water. "My grandfather reached out to me after I left the hospital."

She glanced over at him, her hair falling around her shoulder on one side as she stood up. "No. What happened?"

"I told him to fuck off."

"Conrad."

"Yeah, he died three months later. I just… I knew I was being a dick but I just wasn't ready to forgive him at all. I didn't know he'd die—in fact I would have put money on him being too stubborn to, but he did and…"

He wanted her to know the worst sides of him. She knew about the fight and how he'd almost killed with his fists the man who'd attacked Rory. When he crossed a line and became an asshole, he did it in a big way.

"It's okay," she said. "I mean for him, reaching out to you was probably enough to make him feel better about everything. He could say he tried. Which might have brought him peace when he was dying."

"Maybe." He didn't care about the past except for how it was making him feel about Indy. He walked over to the tub and got in first as she turned off the taps before taking the side with the faucet.

"You're saying goodbye, aren't you?"

"Am I obvious?"

"Yes. I could feel it on the street. What happened to change your mind?" she asked.

"You."

"Me? I swear to God you better give me more than a one-word answer or else," she said.

His arms ached with the need to pull her into them. He wanted her in his heart and in his life, but he wasn't sure he could do it. Be the man she needed. He had held out the television studio and the restaurant as an olive branch. Look at me and see the good things I'm doing. But he'd done them to impress her. For her.

"Fine, the truth is that I hate who I am in this town—I don't mind being a Gilbert out in the world because it's just my last name. Here it comes with baggage, not just mine but the townspeople's too. I watched you tonight, and you love who you are here. This place—"

"Isn't more important than you," she said interrupting him.

She pushed her legs along the sides of his and gave him a smile that felt a bit sad. "You let your guard down with me. Not all the time, but I saw hints of who you would have been if your parents hadn't died and your grandfather hadn't been who he was and—"

"I hadn't lived my life?"

"Ironic I know. But there is a very sweet man underneath that arrogance and that strength that you use to intimidate people and keep them from getting too close. I thought I saw you trying to let that side of yourself out, but then I accepted that you can't."

He wasn't sure he liked where she was going with this. He hadn't realized how much of himself he'd let Indy see or how observant she'd been. But he shouldn't' be surprised. From the beginning she'd seen past the bluster to the man beneath it.

"That man wouldn't have survived the loss that you've experienced. You need that tough thorny exterior—it's the only thing that's keeping you together and letting you live your life."

"I'm not fragile."

She tilted her head. "Not in the way that most people think of that word, but you do have a softness to you. I think I might be one of a handful of people who have seen it. That's what I saw that I wanted to believe in."

"I'm not two men, lady. I'm one. Both of those parts of me exist together, the same way that you have your fiercely driven side and that private side. We can't be just one thing and we can't change to please someone else."

She pulled her legs back, resting her head on her knees. "I wouldn't want to change who I am. I like me. I like you too, Conrad. I don't want to change any of you."

"Not even the part that is leaving in the morning."

"Not even that. That's your choice. I don't like it, but I can't change you."

She put her forehead down on her knees hiding her face to him and he saw her shoulders shake and then she lifted her head.

"I wish—

"Don't. You're not a wishing man. You've never

lied to me. Please don't start now. If you want to leave, I won't stop you."

He got out of the tub and walked out of the room and out of her life without another word.

Fifteen

Conrad had vacillated between coming tonight and staying away. But the truth was, he missed Indy. He'd regretted leaving the moment he'd done it. He'd thought he was doing what was right for her. He was still uncertain what was right for Indy, but he hadn't had anyone to call his own since his parents had died in that plane crash all those years ago.

Indy had been right when she'd said that he wasn't keeping himself safe with the thorns he had tattooed all over his body, covering the scars of the past and the man he'd been. He'd buried himself in the kitchen, found a world where it was okay to be rude, mean and let his temper fly. As the head chef he was the king and everyone had to obey him. Except that had been a false reality. He'd hidden himself in the kitchen away from the real world and the pain it offered.

He'd refused his grandfather's olive branch because he didn't want to reconcile with the man who'd made so many years of his life hell. He'd wanted the old man to die with that on his conscience. And he had held on to that hate as if it were a real thing. Tied it to the town of Gilbert Corners and walked righteously away.

But Indy with her chaotic energy and good heart had somehow found her way past the thorns and anger he'd always used to protect himself. He'd left her because he thought she'd be safer but that was an illusion he no longer could buy into. Indy was stronger than he was with all of his height and muscles and bad ass attitude. She had a strength to be shown the worst part of humanity and decide to create a safe, happy haven for others.

Her show wasn't just something she'd done to figure out where she wanted to go. That show was the essence of the woman he'd come to love. It was her way of showing the world that even in an imperfect world home was what you made of it. And he wanted to make a home with Indy. She'd shown him she wanted that too. Now he had to do the thing he'd never believed he could. He had to open his heart and trust someone else. It had never been easy…

Until Indy.

So he'd thrown this party in her honor and hoped she'd come.

He wanted her back. Not just for a night or few weekends but forever.

A part of him must have known that when he brought her for the weekend, he'd won. He'd struggled to keep her from seeing too much of who he was. Then pushed her away once she had seen the real man.

He wouldn't blame her if she rejected him. She might not want him anymore. It had been two weeks since he'd left. Two weeks when he'd pretended that she was nothing and he wouldn't come back to GC.

"Are you going to just stand up here like a creeper?" Dash asked coming up next to him on the balcony.

"Fuck off."

"No. That's not happening anymore. I've let you keep everyone at bay with your reputation and gruffness but that stops now. You're not that man. I'm not sure that you ever were."

"I beat a man in this very house," he reminded his cousin.

"To avenge my sister. Con, you were never the monster that Grandfather painted you as. He thought he saw himself in you, but the truth is you aren't him. You never were." Dash pulled him back from the edge and hugged him.

He hugged his cousin back. "I'm not sure you're right. I hurt Indy and all she did was ask me to be real with her."

"You were protecting her," Dash said.

"Yes. I just don't want anyone else I love to be hurt."

"Who else have you let down?"

"Well Rory. I should have gotten to her sooner," Conrad said.

"It's easy to look at that night now and try to reconstruct it, but she was headstrong and wanted to date Declan. Nothing either of us said would have stopped her from being young and enjoying the ball. The one to blame is Declan who didn't listen when she said no. I wish that weren't the truth. But you're not to blame for what happened."

"I am a lot like the old man," Conrad said at last.

"The old man would never have thought to throw a gala to win back his woman."

"She likes these kinds of big gestures," Conrad said. He'd realized that the only way he was going to have a chance at getting Indy back was to return to Gilbert Corners and become part of the town she loved.

This was the hardest thing he'd ever had to do, but Indy was worth it. It had been hard to convince the Main Street Business Alliance to agree to a gala up here at the manor and keep his involvement quiet from Indy. But he had wanted the entire night to be a surprise for her. Magical, like she'd thought the ballroom was on that long ago afternoon.

So he'd done it. He was opening a restaurant in town in the next six months, and he had talked Ophelia into using some of the space in the old factory as a filming studio for his *Beast's Lair* show and had made space for Indy's *Hometown, Home Again* show to have production space as well. But that all meant nothing if Indy didn't forgive him and take him back.

He knew she cared about him. But second chances weren't something that many people gave when it came to relationships. Would she take a chance on him again?

Hell.

He was going to have to leave the balcony and see if she'd come to the party.

Two weeks passed, and as Labor Day weekend approached, Indy gave up all hope of Conrad coming back to Gilbert Corners. The Main Street Business Alliance was happy with the increase in foot traffic to the town. The old factory was going to be opening up again as a combined retail and entertainment space, which made everyone happy.

In fact, the town of Gilbert Corners was on its way to becoming everything that Indy had thought she wanted. Well, she still wanted it, but she wasn't enjoying it. And tonight felt even worse because she had been invited to a formal charity gala at Gilbert Manor. She hadn't been back there since her weekend with Conrad.

It was hard not to see him everywhere she went. It wasn't like he'd been in her shop but still, she saw him there, imagined his broad shoulders filling the doorway. In fact, every time the bell tinkled and the door opened, she glanced up with some hope in her heart that he'd come back.

But he hadn't.

He wasn't a man to do things halfway. When he'd walked out the door, that was it. She knew it. He'd given her back her hope and her confidence as a woman. She could now look back on dating Wayne and see that she'd used him to hide from having to trust again. She'd called her old boyfriend and thanked him for giving her that. He admitted he hadn't known what to do but had wanted to help her. And Indy appreciated that.

It was only after being with Conrad that she could see how she'd been so focused on the pain and stuck in her fear to really move on. But it was also Gilbert Corners and Nola's friendship that had helped heal her.

"We don't have to go," Nola said as they both were sharing the mirror in the bathroom at the bookshop.

Indy leaned in to put on her eyeliner. "I feel like since it's a thank-you for getting Conrad to come here, I can't not go."

"Yeah, I guess. Not that it did much good."

She shook her head in the mirror and turned to face her friend. "It did so. You don't have to be mad at him because he doesn't want a relationship with me."

"Girl, you're my ride or die—I am always going to have your back," Nola said.

"You're mine," she said, hugging Nola and feeling that twinge of sadness come close to overwhelming her. Turned out she wasn't like her mom. Love had just made her more determined to follow her dreams. She'd had a chance at love and it had walked away. She didn't have to worry about losing herself to Conrad because he wasn't willing to let her in.

Which was totally his prerogative. She knew that and respected it. But she was still mad, and also still in love with him. It seemed one of the great injustices of the universe that love wasn't automatically a two-way emotion. Why had she been willing to take the risk when he hadn't?

She swallowed, forced a smile and finished putting on her makeup. She was going to fake being okay until she was. Fake being happy with breaking the curse even though doing so had brought her heartache. Fake being her best self because that's what both she and the town needed.

"I'm surprised that Dash agreed to have the gala at the manor," Nola said.

"Me too. But it is a beautiful space and really should be used." She steeled herself against going into that ballroom again. Even in her memories she still got turned on from standing on the balcony and kissing Conrad. Those moments were etched in her mind. Maybe she should back out.

"It is. Wow, you look like a princess tonight," Nola said. "I've never seen you this dressed up."

"I was a Southern deb and can look nice," she retorted.

But she had pulled out all the stops tonight ordering a custom gown from the seamstress back in Lansdowne so it would fit her perfectly. The fitted bodice hugged her curves and then flowed out from her waist in a fall of tulle that ended at the floor. Her shoes were Manolo because they were her favorite, and she wore the tiara her mother had given her when she turned sixteen. She also had diamond studs that had been her great-aunt's.

Nola was dressed in a tux with a bright pink tie. She'd died one strand of her red hair a bright fuchsia and had done her eyeliner and mascara heavy. Honestly, Nola always was the most eye-catching person which was one of the reasons why Indy loved her. Nola never hid her light, she let it shine.

And Indy wanted that.

Actually, she'd found that. She might be sad that Conrad couldn't love her, but she wasn't broken or less-than because he didn't.

"Yeah, I didn't mean it bad. It's just I'm used to you in your glasses and cardigan in the bookshop. This is next-level. I feel like a schlub next to you."

"Don't be ridiculous. You always look gorgeous. I have no doubt that people will not even notice me when we both walk in," she said to her friend.

"Ha. Ready to storm the manor?"

"Nothing daunts me—I'm the curse breaker."

Nola laughed and when the Uber dropped them off in the porte cochere of Gilbert Manor, they both linked arms. "Thank you for coming with me tonight."

"Like I said, ride or die," Nola responded.

The foyer was decked out for the party with lights and a string quartet playing Vivaldi's *Spring* from *The Four Seasons*. There were waiters carrying trays with champagne and Nola took two glasses before handing one to Indy.

Indy lifted hers to toast her friend when she felt someone watching her and looked up to see Conrad standing on the landing looking down. She tried to be cool and smile at him, but couldn't. She still loved him, and it was heartbreaking to see him again this soon.

He put his hand on the banister and started walking down it just as she looked up. Their eyes met and his heartbeat became faster, his cock hardened and his mind went blank. God, she was gorgeous.

He'd missed her so much and thought he remembered every detail of how she looked, but he saw now that he'd forgotten about that tiny birthmark next to her ear. And exactly how full her mouth was.

Whatever it took, he was going to win her back. He was the Beast and this was his lair, and he wasn't about to lose, not now when the stakes were so high and he'd found the love he hadn't known he'd been craving all of his life.

He went down the rest of the stairs as she turned her back on him and linked her arm through Nola's starting to walk away.

"Indy."

She stopped, looking back over her shoulder at him, her chin held high as she stared at him.

"Yes."

"Can I speak with you privately?"

She chewed her lower lip, which gave him hope and then she nodded and stepped away from Nola.

Conrad held his hand out to her and led her through the foyer and back up the stairs, toward the balcony over the ballroom. He looked so good in the tuxedo that she was tempted to just pretend that everything was okay. But that was old Indy and she couldn't do that anymore.

She stopped walking and pulled her hand free of his. "What are you doing here?"

"I live here," he said.

"Since when?"

"Since Wednesday. I came back here for you, Indy."

What? Surprise, followed quickly by excitement then doubt. "Why?"

He shook his head. "You have every right to question my motives. Will you come with me to the ballroom, let me explain it to you there?"

She was tempted to say no but knew that was just her lingering anger from the way he'd left. "Yes, but first you have to tell what's going on."

"I…"

For the first time ever he was at a loss for words. That startled her. What was going on? What did he mean he lived here?

"Conrad—"

He put his finger over her lips to stop her speaking, a shiver of awareness went through her and she closed her eyes for a moment steeling herself to be strong.

"You were right. I was pretending to protect myself, using my anger at my grandfather to keep everyone at bay."

She smiled at him. "I'm glad you realized that. You know you don't have to do that. There are a lot of people who care about you."

"I don't really need *a lot of people* to care about me, lady. I just need you," he said. "I know I messed up, and given your past and the trust you placed in me, I really let you down. That wasn't my intention."

She realized she was holding her breath and reminded herself to believe. This was Conrad and she loved him and she couldn't help hoping that he might have realized he loved her too.

"I know you didn't mean to hurt me," she said.

"Thanks for that. I love you. I'm probably still

going to fuck up—that's who I am. But it won't be because I don't care. I've moved back here. I'm living here now. I'm opening a restaurant. And I want the chance to start again. Will you start again with me?"

She wasn't entirely sure she believed her ears but for the love she saw shining in his eyes and the sincerity in his voice. If she knew one thing about Conrad Gilbert it was that he didn't say things to be nice. He loved her.

"I love you," she said. "I don't think I'll be perfect but I'm pretty sure that relationships aren't supposed to be perfect. I think they are just supposed to be togetherness. Someone to laugh with, share fears with and hold in the middle of the night."

Conrad gathered her into his arms lifting her off her feet, before kissing her deeply. In the distance she heard the band start playing and the sound of voices chattering away in the ballroom. Conrad set her down and led her to the balcony of the ballroom.

They entered on the dark cloudy side. "This was the day we met. Remember the storm blowing, the competition and the wager?"

"I do," she said.

He led her around to the lightening skies which were transition to a night sky and the fiber-optic stars began to twinkle. "This is where we are now. A new day, a new beginning. Will you marry me and spend the rest of your life with me?"

She looked up at him, to the scar that ran down one side of his face, his full masculine lips and then lower where the thorny branches of his tattoo were visible, and she leaned in closer, noticing something she hadn't before. There were tiny rosebuds on the branches.

"Did you do this for me?"

"I did Rosalinda. Figured I might as well put you in ink since you were already in my heart."

"Oh, dear beast."

"You haven't answered my question," he reminded her, pulling her into his arms, then resting his forehead against hers.

"Yes. I'll marry you."

He kissed her then and she heard the sound of applause from the ballroom below. When she lifted her head a few minutes later the orchestra was playing and everyone was dancing. She and her beast made their way down the stairs and into the ballroom.

* * * * *